ANNA IS STILL HERE

Anna sits up in bed. The light goes on. Anna would like to put her hands over her face, but she doesn't dare. Blood would get in her eyes.

"Anna, what's the matter?" Her mother is at her bedside. She sits down next to Anna. "Anna dear, what's the matter?"

"Marga, a bang . . . blood." She looks at her mother.

"So you know about Marga? We didn't want to tell you that she's dead, but now you know, anyway."

Anna pulls the blanket over her head. She never wants to come out again.

"This terse translation from the Dutch is compelling in its simplicity. . . . It is a stark reminder that the effects of the Holocaust did not end with the end of the war."

— School Library Journal

"There's no idealization—anti-Semitism isn't dead [after World War II]; even those who saved the Jews included some 'stupid heroes'—but with the anger and sorrow there's also courage." *— Booklist*

Anna Is Still Here

Ida Vos

Translated by Terese Edelstein
and Inez Smidt

SCHOLASTIC INC.
New York Toronto London Auckland Sydney

For Henk, who has known Anna since her birth,
and for Josephine, Karel, and Bert, who will
recognize her

ISBN 0-590-60228-4

12 11 10 9 8 7 6 5 4 3 2 1   5 6 7 8 9/9 0/0

Printed in the U.S.A.   40

First Scholastic printing, December 1995

✦ Heinrich

Anna Markus knows it for sure. A German soldier has stayed behind in the white house on the water. There were many German soldiers in the white house four weeks ago, when Anna was still in hiding, but they've all been captured now. All except for Heinrich.

Anna knows exactly what Heinrich looks like. He has a helmet on his head and he has steel-blue eyes.

Heinrich came to the Netherlands in 1940 to occupy the country, and there he remained. For five long years Heinrich and his comrades told the Dutch people what to do. Then suddenly the German occupation was over. A swastika flag is no longer hanging from the white house. Soldiers are no longer going in and out. Heinrich is all alone. He never goes outside. Anna knows that today or tomorrow he will no longer be able to stand being all by himself. One day, naturally when Anna must walk past the house on her way to school, he will come storming outside. He will grab her and drag her into the house.

"So, Anna," he will hiss through his teeth. "I finally have you, Anna. You were hiding from us up in the attic room for a long time, but I've got you at last. I'll take you to Germany, to my country. I'll flee from Holland and I'll take you with me. You see, Anna, I still hate Jewish children, especially thirteen-year-old girls!"

Anna often dreams about Heinrich. She sees him sitting before the window of the white house. She sees the filthy curtains and the windowsill with the dead plants on it. The plants have fingers that want to pull her inside. She awakens screaming and soaking with sweat. When her father and mother ask why she is screaming, she says that she doesn't know. She doesn't dare tell anyone about her dream. If her parents should keep on asking, maybe she would tell them about it. But only a little.

Anna must go past the white house today. Yesterday she walked by with her eyes closed, but she nearly bumped into a tree. She will keep her eyes open today and just glance at the house, perhaps. Sometimes she really is a bit curious about Heinrich.

Anna walks by the house with one eye open and one eye closed. At least she will be able to see the tree now. She stops for a moment. She sees the dirty curtains.

"No!" she screams, and runs away. Faster . . . faster. The filthy curtains moved. She saw Heinrich's hand.

Anna can't run any farther, for she has a pain in her side. But she hears the sound of Heinrich's boots behind her. He is going to get her. Too late! She wasn't quick enough. Heinrich can run very fast.

Anna begins to run again, and she keeps running until she reaches school. She rings the bell. Yuri, a sixth grader, opens the door for her.

"Your class is singing," he says. "Hurry up."

Anna carefully opens the door to her fifth-grade classroom. Miss De Wit looks at her.

"You're late, Anna," she says. "You weren't in hiding again, were you?"

A few children begin to snicker.

Anna doesn't laugh.

◆ Anna Can't Sleep

Anna is angry at her parents. Why don't they tell her what happened to everyone during the war? Where is Uncle Bernard? Where is Aunt Geertje and where is Marga? Marga is her best friend, and she hasn't seen her in such a long time. Where is she?

When Anna lies in bed at night, she hears her parents talking. At first she hears a sort of buzzing sound, but if

she listens closely she hears names. Bergen-Belsen . . .
Theresienstadt. Why don't her parents talk louder?

Anna keeps listening for Marga's name. "Marga, where
are you?" she sometimes says aloud.

Marga doesn't reply. Anna can't help crying then, for
Marga isn't there.

She feels free to cry only when she is under the covers.
Then no one can see her and no one can hear her.

Anna dreams:

She is standing in the garden, in the snow. Her feet are
bare. The sun and the moon are in the sky at the same
time. Anna looks up and sees something very peculiar. A
red balloon is floating about, and someone in a white
dress is hanging from a red string underneath it. The balloon drops down a little. Now Anna can see that a girl is
hanging from the string. Marga!

She reaches out to Marga. Marga takes Anna's hand
and they float upward, toward the sun and the moon.
The girls can't talk to each other, but they can laugh together.

"Come back down to earth with me," Anna says.
Marga doesn't answer.

High above them is a bird, a big black bird. It has a
sharp beak. Anna keeps looking at the bird. Doesn't
Marga see it?

The bird is above the balloon now. It stretches its claws
and reaches out with its beak.

"No!" Anna cries.

A bursting sound. The bird has pierced the balloon. Marga falls down below. Anna remains in the air.

A bird is flying next to her, a white bird. Anna tries to drift away from it, but the bird flies underneath her.

"No!" Anna shouts. "Don't!"

Her arms and legs are becoming heavy. She is going to crash!

Anna lets herself fall, but feels that she is being held back. She looks down and sees that she is sitting upon white feathers. The bird has caught her. Carefully it flies toward the earth. Carefully it sets her down in the snow, next to Marga.

"Marga," Anna says softly. She takes Marga's hand. The hand is cold. A piece of balloon is resting in the middle of it. Anna picks up the balloon. It becomes warm. It becomes liquid. It begins to flow.

"Blood!" screams Anna. "Blood!"

She sits up in bed. The light goes on. Anna would like to put her hands over her face, but she doesn't dare. Blood would get in her eyes.

"Anna, what's the matter?" Her mother is at her bedside. She sits down next to Anna. "Anna dear, what's the matter?"

"Marga, a bang . . . blood." She looks at her mother.

"So you know about Marga? We didn't want to tell you that she's dead, but now you know, anyway."

Anna pulls the blanket over her head. She never wants to come out again.

Someone is pulling on the blanket. "Get out from under the covers, Anna!"

Papa is now in her room, too.

"No!" Anna shouts. "You liars. You with your quiet talk. You can both go to hell!"

"What's the matter with her?" she hears her father ask.

"She knows about Marga. She is all upset."

Anna hears a strange noise. Slowly she pulls the blanket away. Her parents are sitting on the floor in front of the bed, weeping. Anna climbs out of bed and sits down on the floor next to them.

"Don't cry. Don't cry," she says. She can't stand to see grown-ups cry.

"There is a photograph of Marga in a drawer downstairs. Shall we set it out?" her mother says, trying to comfort her.

"Judith, please!" her father shouts. "Don't. Please, no photos of murdered people."

"How did you know about Marga?" Mama has to blow her nose all of a sudden.

"I don't know."

"Did you . . ."

"I really don't know."

Anna stands up. Her mother and father are still sitting on the floor.

"You don't have to talk so quietly in the evenings anymore," she tells them. "I know everything now."

✦ Who Is H. Neumann?

"Anna, are you coming with us to the Draaikolk this afternoon?" Martijn asks.

"No," Anna says.

"Why not? It's Wednesday. We don't have school on Wednesday afternoon."

Anna doesn't reply. How can she possibly tell Martijn that the reason she doesn't want to go to the amusement park is because she would have to walk past the white house again?

"Well, why not?" Martijn gives her a push.

"I . . . I . . . it's too expensive. I want to go, but we can't afford it."

"Tell me the truth!" Martijn pushes her again.

"Because . . . because a Nazi lives in the white house along the way. A Nazi has stayed behind there."

"*What?*"

"A Nazi. A German soldier. His name is Heinrich."

Martijn bursts out laughing. "Boys, did you hear that? Anna says that there is a Nazi living in the white house."

"I . . . I've seen him myself," Anna stutters. "Last week, on my way to school."

"What did he look like?"

"His hand . . . I saw his hand."

"Just his hand?" Martijn is surprised. "You're coming

with us, Anna. Marion and Pieter and I will pick you up at one o'clock this afternoon."

Anna must go along with the other children. At five minutes to one Martijn is standing at the door, together with Pieter and Marion.

"Have a good time," says Mama.

"Humph," Anna replies.

"We'll ring the doorbell as soon as we get to the white house," says Pieter, "and then we'll see what will happen."

"No!" Anna wants to turn back.

Marion grabs hold of her. "Don't be so stupid. Who's afraid of just one Nazi?"

"*I* am," Anna says.

They are at the white house now.

"Look, there's a name plate on the door," Martijn whispers. "Let's see what's on it. Are you coming?"

"I'll stay here by the gate," says Anna.

Martijn, Pieter, and Marion walk to the door. "'Neumann,'" Pieter reads aloud. "'H. Neumann.'"

"There's another name. Two people live here," Marion whispers. "Look: 'H. Neumann — Erika van Waardenberg.' Anna is right. A Nazi *does* live here. That letter H. stands for Heinrich, of course, and Erika must be his girlfriend."

"Don't be an idiot, Marion," Pieter says. "Do you honestly think that someone who wants to hide will put his name on the door? Come on, let's ring the bell." He pulls the copper doorbell. The door remains closed.

"There's no one home!" calls Marion.

"There is, too!" shouts Anna. "Look up at the window."

"Darn," says Pieter. "The curtain *is* moving."

"See? Heinrich's hand." Anna can barely talk.

"We'll ring the bell again," says Marion.

Heinrich's hand has disappeared. The door opens, and a woman appears. She is wearing a black dress with blue flowers on it. Her hair is uncombed. "What do you want?" she asks.

"The Nazi, where is the Nazi?" shouts Martijn.

"Nazi? What Nazi?" asks the woman.

"The one who lives here."

"A Nazi . . . here? Are you *crazy*? There's no Nazi here."

"Who is H. Neumann?" Pieter shouts.

"I am," says the woman.

"And Erika van Waardenberg?"

"I'm Erika van Waardenberg, too." She slams the door.

"Crazy fat woman," says Martijn. "Do you know what I think, Anna? That's not a Nazi you've seen, it's a witch. She was looking at you, Anna. Ha, that witch looks at Anna every time she passes the house on her way to school!" He slaps Anna on her backside. "Come on, walk. To the Draaikolk."

Anna walks with the others, but she would much

rather go home. She still feels certain that Heinrich lives in the white house. This woman Erika is his girlfriend, and she doesn't want to betray him. That's the truth of the matter.

When they arrive at the Draaikolk, Martijn and Pieter run to the slide. Marion goes on the swings. Anna doesn't know what to do. She doesn't enjoy going down the slide, and swinging makes her sick to her stomach. She stands alone and watches the others.

"Say, do you know where the puppet show is?"

Anna feels someone pulling on her sleeve. A little girl is looking up at her. "No, but shall we look for it together?" Anna asks the child.

The little girl takes hold of Anna's hand. "What's your name?"

"Anna, and yours?"

"Corrie."

"Where do you live, Corrie?"

"Far away, in Brabant. My mama says that the Draaikolk is the biggest amusement park in Holland, and that's why we've come here."

"Look, Corrie, there's the puppet show. Come on, let's sit down on a bench."

Corrie is still holding Anna by the hand. Anna finds that quite pleasant. She doesn't need to do anything else now. "I have to stay with Corrie," is what she will tell Pieter and Martijn when they come to nag her because she is afraid of everything.

"Where is the landlord?" calls the puppet Katrijn.

"Here!" shouts Jan Klaassen. "And here comes someone else!"

"Ha, ha, ha. I am the witch." Another puppet appears.

Corrie squeezes Anna's hand. Anna is frightened, too. That witch . . . she looks like Erika van Waardenberg. Anna doesn't want to think about it.

"I'm leaving, Corrie," she whispers. "Stay in your seat."

"I'm going home," Anna tells Pieter and Martijn, who are playing on the seesaw.

Pieter looks at Anna. "You think you're too big, don't you? Thirteen years old and only in the fifth grade. You think you're too old to play with us, don't you? Then beat it!"

Marion is standing by the seesaw, too. "You're mean!" she calls. "You know perfectly well that Anna can't help being in the fifth grade. If you had been in hiding for three years, you would probably be in the second grade. I'll go with you, Anna. Come on."

Together they walk out the gate.

"Stupid girls!" Pieter calls. "Stupid girls!"

◆ Refugee

As Anna walks past the white house she notices that something strange is taking place there, something that she hasn't seen before. The door is open.

Anna looks in and sees a long hallway. The floor is made of marble. "It's happened," Anna says to herself. "Erika and Heinrich have fled and they didn't have time to shut the door."

She doesn't have to be afraid anymore. She can take her time when she walks to school now. Being late for school isn't so bad.

She walks slowly. The weather is warm. Flowers are blooming in all the gardens. Boats are sailing past. People are waving from a big ship.

"Hello!" Anna calls. "Hello, everybody!" She begins to skip. It feels wonderful to be outside without a jacket.

She hears footsteps behind her; she doesn't need to look back, for she is no longer afraid. The footsteps get faster . . . faster.

"I've got you!"

Someone has grabbed her by the shoulder. Anna turns around. "No!" she cries. "Don't, Erika. Let me go!"

"Calm down," says the woman. "Calm down. I'm not going to hurt you."

Anna tries to free herself by hitting Erika's arm, but Erika is holding her tightly.

"Hit me," Erika says. "Hit me. I won't feel a thing through my winter coat."

"I'm not going to Germany!" Anna shouts. "You and Heinrich go by yourselves!"

"My girl, listen for a moment. I have something to explain to you."

"You don't have to." Anna has freed herself from the woman's grasp. "I have to go to school."

"I told you there was no Heinrich in my house the time you came to my door with those other children. Come look. I'll let you see my whole house."

"There is, too! H. Neumann lives with you. Heinrich Neumann."

"*I* am H. Neumann. The letter H. stands for Henriette, not Heinrich. Please believe me."

"Neumann is a German name, and you speak with a German accent."

"That's right, my girl, that's right. I'm from Germany, but I fled to Holland in 1937. The Jews in Germany were already in great danger then."

Anna looks at the woman. "Are you Jewish?" she asks. She almost said, "I am, too," but she doesn't dare. Perhaps the woman is lying about everything. Perhaps she wants to lock Anna up in the white house, after all.

"And what about Erika van Waardenberg?"

"I'm Erika van Waardenberg, too. It was my name when I was in hiding. We had to take other names when we were in hiding. Come inside. I have a lot more to tell you."

"No," Anna whispers.

The woman doesn't hear her. She looks at Anna. She puts her hand on Anna's head.

"Don't," says Anna, but the woman's hand remains on Anna's head.

"The spitting image . . ." she whispers. "The spitting image. That's why I followed you . . . that's why."

Anna is frightened. "I have to go to school," she says.

"Go ahead," says the woman. "Do your best." She releases Anna. "Will you wave to me? What is your name?"

"Anna, Anna Markus."

"Pretty name. Will you wave to me, Anna?"

"All right."

The woman stands and waves. She has taken off her coat. She is wearing the blue-flowered dress. "Goodbye, Anna!" she calls. "Goodbye, Anna, see you later!"

"I don't know about that," Anna says.

◆ *Kiki*

Kiki is much nicer than any of the other children Anna knows. Nicer than Vera, nicer than Martijn, nicer than Marion. Anna can talk about difficult things with Kiki. About people who are still alive, about people who were killed.

Anna and Kiki can play checkers very well together. It goes something like this:

"What do you want to be, Kiki? Red or black?"

"I want to be red, Anna."

"You always want to be red, Kiki. Let's draw lots."

"Never mind. I'll be black."

"Okay."

Sometimes Anna and Kiki quarrel. Anna finds Kiki very unpleasant then, and she says to her, "Kiki, I think you're rotten. I don't want to be your friend anymore."

"That's all right with me. I'll just get myself another friend."

During the war, Kiki was the only person who was allowed to see Anna up in the attic room, and Kiki never told anyone about those visits.

"That's nice of you, Kiki," Anna said. "It's nice that you never betrayed me when I was up in Mr. De Bree's attic."

"Of course I didn't betray you, Anna. You're my friend, aren't you?" Kiki answered.

They took long trips together, even when Anna was in hiding. They went everywhere. They set foot on all the continents of the world.

They went to Turkey and to Persia. They saw mummies in Egypt, and in Central Java they saw a temple called the Borobudur.

They talked about their travels for days on end. For weeks.

They also wrote a story together about Prince William of Orange, who was assassinated in Delft. They both wept bitterly over poor Prince William.

Nowadays Anna doesn't see Kiki as often as she used to; but sometimes Kiki appears quite suddenly, when Anna feels lonely or afraid.

"Do you know this joke, Anna?" Kiki will say, and she will then do her best to make Anna laugh. She usually succeeds, too. Laughing and crying, Anna and Kiki do that together.

Kiki is the nicest child in the whole world. Nicer than Vera, nicer than Martijn, nicer than Marion.

If only Kiki really did exist!

✦ Rain at Last

Even though it's raining when Anna comes out of school, she doesn't put her coat on. She had yearned for rain for such a very long time, up in the attic room.

While in hiding she had made a list of things she wanted to do after she was free. At the top of the list was: "Walk in the rain." Her second wish was: "Walk in the sun."

When you have wanted it to rain *that* badly, you certainly aren't going to put on your coat when it finally does rain! Anna is soaking wet, and she finds it wonderful.

She passes by the white house on the Vlietkade. She glances up and notices that the curtains are not moving. Surely Mrs. Neumann is not at home.

Anna hears a noise coming from the garden, a very soft one. It sounds like someone crying. She enters through the gate and walks toward the sound, which is coming from the rhododendron bush. As Anna approaches the bush, the sound becomes louder.

She kneels down. "Oh, how sweet," she says. A cat is sitting there under the bush.

"Here, kitty kitty!"

Two blue eyes look out at Anna.

"Here, kitty kitty, don't be afraid." She wiggles her fingers to attract the cat's attention. It crawls out from under the rhododendron.

"Come on." Anna picks up the cat and puts her cheek against its head. How soft it is! Anna looks up at the second story window. Nothing is moving behind the dead plants.

What is Anna to do? She doesn't dare ring the doorbell.

"Are you coming with me, kitty? Are you coming with me? Let's go!"

The cat begins to purr.

"Yes, I hear you. You *do* want to come. Shall I tell you something? I had a cat before we went into hiding. His name was Maupie. Before we had to leave home, I brought him to some Gentile people, and when I got there and opened the cat carrier, he ran away. That was terrible, wasn't it?"

A tear falls on the cat's head.

"That's why I'm taking you with me. Then I'll have a cat again."

Anna walks out of the garden. She covers the cat with her coat, otherwise it will become very wet.

Suddenly Anna stands still. What if this cat belongs to Mrs. Neumann? Anna can't just take it away, can she? What should she do?

The cat is moving under her coat. Anna can feel it purring on her chest. She takes a few more steps, then walks back to the house. She decides to put the cat down under the rhododendron bush. Mrs. Neumann can certainly find it then. Slowly she returns to the garden. She kneels down again.

"Go under the bush, kitty, and wait for Mrs. Neumann."

The cat sets its claws in Anna's sweater.

"Ouch, don't do that. Under the bush you go." She sets the cat under the rhododendron, then stands up.

The cat begins to meow again, louder than before.

"Don't," says Anna. "Don't start that again. Well, let's go. I'll ring the doorbell. Only because you're a cat and can't ring the doorbell yourself."

Anna pulls on the bell. The loud ring startles her. She hears movement upstairs. A window opens.

"Who is it?"

"Me . . . I mean, your cat." Anna wants to run away.

"My cat? Wait a minute." Mrs. Neumann disappears, but returns after a moment.

"Amalia certainly isn't in her basket. Wait, I'm coming."

Again Anna wants to run away, but the door is already open.

"Amalia!" Mrs. Neumann calls. "Amalia!"

Slowly the cat crawls out from under the rhododendron.

"How nice that you found Amalia," says Mrs. Neumann. "Would you like to come in? Oh, don't you want to? Well, then I'll go get you a piece of candy, real American candy. I have a brother who lives in the United States, and he sent me a package filled with candy and clothes and chewing gum. And do you know what else was in it? Stockings, strange stockings. They aren't made of wool or silk, but of nylon. Do you know what nylon is?"

"No, I don't," Anna replies. "Aren't you going to visit your brother in the United States someday?"

Mrs. Neumann doesn't reply. She looks at Anna without really seeing her.

"I can't go to the United States," she says quietly. "I can't ever leave. Fannie could come. I'm waiting for Fannie. For weeks I've been waiting for Fannie."

✦ Shouting

"Louder, Anna, I can't understand you."

"What did you say, Anna? You're allowed to talk again. You're no longer all by yourself in the attic room."

Anna finds it unpleasant when her mother and father ask her to speak loudly. She doesn't yet dare to do it. She didn't talk to anyone for almost three years. Whom are you to talk to when you're all alone? To Kiki or to yourself, but that gets boring after a while. It was only when Mr. De Bree came to bring her meal to her that she would speak: "Thank you, Mr. De Bree."

"Enjoy your food, child," Mr. De Bree would answer, and after he had spoken, he would let his cigar move from the one corner of his mouth to the other. When he had finished doing that, he would go back downstairs. To give trumpet lessons.

"I have an idea," Papa says. "Each morning we'll go to the dunes, Anna. There is a section where we're allowed to go. There aren't any more land mines there. We can shout together on the dunes. No one will be able to hear us. In this way I'll teach you how to open your mouth again."

"I don't want to," says Anna.

"Well, we're going, anyway," her father answers.

✦   ✦   ✦

They are at the dunes, dressed in their raincoats and boots. It is still cold. Soon the sun will be higher and the weather will have warmed up a bit.

"I'll go stand over there," her father says, pointing in the distance. "And then I'll ask you something. You'll have to talk loudly, Anna, otherwise I won't be able to hear you."

Her father walks away. When he is far enough from Anna he stops and turns toward her.

"What time is it, Anna?" she hears him shout.

"Six o'clock!" she calls.

"What did you say, Anna?"

"Six o'clock!"

"I can't understand you. Louder. You'll have to shout!"

Anna does her best to shout very loudly, but not a sound comes out of her throat.

"Come on, Anna!" her father yells.

Anna lets herself sink down to the sand. She doesn't want to shout.

Papa comes back to her. He strokes her head. "It doesn't matter," he says, comforting her. "We'll try again tomorrow, and the day after tomorrow. You'll see, the day will come when you can shout louder than I can. It's no wonder that you can't shout. A thirteen-year-old girl who didn't speak for almost three years. And now you have to, all of a sudden."

He raises a clenched fist up high. "Rotten Nazis!" he cries. "Look what you've done to my child!"

"Don't," says Anna. Not only is she afraid to shout, she is afraid when other people shout, too.

"Today we'll try to shout across the sea," her father says. "Run, Anna!"

Hand in hand, they run toward the North Sea. The weather is stormy and the waves are as high as church towers.

"On the other side is England," her father says. "Who is the King of England?"

"King George."

"Right. Now you call to the King of England and ask him what he wants for breakfast. Go on."

"Do you want toast, Your Highness?" Anna calls.

"Louder, Anna. You can do it."

"Do . . . you . . . want . . . toast . . . Your . . . High . . . ness!"

"Wonderful, Anna. A little louder." Papa is so pleased with her that he is dancing in a puddle of water and splattering mud all over his raincoat.

A man and his dog are walking in the distance. The dog runs up to Anna, sniffs her, and runs back. Then he comes up to Anna again.

She looks at the little tag hanging from his collar. JOHANNES is printed across it.

Anna laughs. A dog named Johannes. A person's name. Johannes runs away. He is quite far from her now.

"Call him," her father says. "You know his name. Go

on. I'll bet he hears you. First we'll call him together and then you call him by yourself."

"Johannes!" they call at the same time.

"Now by yourself, Anna. Do your best."

"Johannes!" she calls. "Johannes!"

The dog comes running toward them at full speed. When he has reached Anna, he stops and licks her face.

"Good dog," Anna whispers.

"Good dog!" she shouts.

"My word, how you can shout." The dog's owner laughs as he approaches them. "What a voice you have, girl. You know, Johannes is a little bit deaf, but he heard you, anyway. That's a miracle. And with this storm, too. Listen to what I have to say, girl. You should go into opera, with such a voice. You should become a singer."

The man looks surprised when Father grabs Anna and nearly tosses her up into the air.

"Don't!" Anna screams. "Don't. I'll fall!"

The man and his dog continue their walk, but Anna can still hear him talking in the distance:

"Johannes, how that girl can shout. I'm glad she's not *my* daughter!"

◆ American Dresses

"Anna!"

Anna looks up. Mrs. Neumann has shoved the plants aside and is leaning out over the windowsill. She has a pink dress on.

"Anna, I want to ask you something. Please come upstairs for a minute."

Anna would rather go home, but Mrs. Neumann is asking in such a special way that she doesn't dare ignore her. Perhaps Mrs. Neumann is sick.

"I'm coming!" Anna calls to her.

"Come in," Mrs. Neumann says.

They walk up a long stairway. It is dark in the upstairs hall. Mrs. Neumann opens the door.

"Go in," she says. "I live here. This is my room, but you knew that because you've seen me standing in front of the window so often."

Anna finds herself in a large room furnished only with a table and a few chairs.

"Pretty, aren't they?" says Mrs. Neumann as she points to a wall. "All from the United States, those dresses."

Anna doesn't know where to look first. There are dresses hanging everywhere, in all sorts of colors: flaming red, yellow, blue.

"Sit down." Mrs. Neumann pulls up a chair for her.

"What were you going to ask me?" Anna says.

"Who . . . me? Was I going to ask you something?"

"Yes, that's what you said when you called down."

"Oh, did I say that? No, I didn't want to ask you anything. I wanted to . . . I just wanted to see you for a little while and I can't go outside today. That's why I asked if you wanted to come upstairs. My dress is in the wash, you see. That's the reason I can't go out."

"Your dress? What about all those dresses, then?" Anna says, pointing to the wall.

Mrs. Neumann shakes her head. "No," she says, "I can't wear those."

"Don't they fit?"

"Yes . . . yes, they fit."

"Then why . . .?"

"Listen, Anna. I *must* wear that dress with the blue flowers on it. Otherwise Fannie won't recognize me when she comes."

Anna stands up. She wants to leave. Mrs. Neumann is acting so strangely.

"Fannie would recognize this nightgown, too. I wore it the last night . . ."

"Who is Fannie?"

"Do you want to know?"

"Yes."

"Fannie is my little daughter. She's seven years old. She was captured, together with her father, but she's coming back. I don't know where she is at the moment, but the people from the Red Cross are looking for her. They're going to find her and bring her here. They know that I live in this house. Now do you understand why I can never leave and why I have to keep wearing that black dress with the blue flowers? Fannie has to be able to recognize my clothes, and I have to be here for her, always."

Mrs. Neumann stands up. She walks to a closet and fetches a little box.

"Hold out your hand, Anna." She puts the box in Anna's hand. "Take a look."

Anna opens it. A small bracelet is lying on a wad of yellow cotton.

"Silver," Mrs. Neumann says. "A bracelet made of silver coins, all from the year 1938. Fannie was born in 1938, on January 31, the same day as Princess Beatrix. All the flags were hanging out. When Fannie comes home, I'm going to give her this bracelet."

The room is quiet. Mrs. Neumann is sitting across from Anna at the table. She looks at Anna. Anna hardly dares to return her gaze.

"I think that red dress is pretty, Mrs. Neumann," she says.

Mrs. Neumann doesn't answer; she keeps looking at Anna. "Get your hair off your face, Anna," she says.

Anna puts a few curls behind her ear.

"The spitting image . . . the spitting image of Fannie. That birthmark on your forehead. Fannie has a birthmark on her forehead, too. It's incredible."

Silence. Mrs. Neumann stares at Anna again.

"Fannie is coming back," she whispers. "And then I'll put on that flaming-red dress. She was arrested, along with Max. And I wasn't there. I had to be away for a little while, and that's why I'm still alive and . . ."

Mrs. Neumann tries to stand, but she groans and falls back into her chair.

"Shall I tell you who won't be coming back?" Saliva oozes from her lips. "Max . . . Max won't be coming back. Fannie will have to go through life without her father. Wait, I'll get the letter from the Red Cross. Then you can see for yourself."

Mrs. Neumann lays an envelope marked with a red cross down on the table. "Here . . . here it is." She slaps the envelope. "Look."

Anna kicks her chair over. She runs away, down the long flight of steps. She doesn't want to look at that envelope. When she has reached the first floor she tries to open the door to the outside.

Mrs. Neumann is standing up above on the landing. "Running away, are you?" she shouts. "When it gets too difficult, you run away. You abandon me . . . all of you. Whenever I want to talk about Max and Fannie, everyone abandons me. Damn you all! You haven't experienced anything! You haven't suffered a bit!"

"That's not true!" Anna shouts angrily. "I've been through a whole lot. I was in hiding, too!"

Anna is finally able to open the door. She runs outside, through the gate.

"Anna!" Mrs. Neumann is leaning out the window again. "Anna! I know that you're going to tell your parents what happened, and then they won't let you come visit me again. Anna?"

"I'm not going to tell them anything!" Anna calls. "They couldn't bear to hear about it. And I'm never coming back. Never!" She keeps walking.

"Come back, Anna. Anna!"

✦ *Telephone*

"Telephone for you, Anna. Someone named Jet."

"Jet?" Anna puts her fork down. "I don't know anyone named Jet."

"She asked for you. Come on." Mother is growing a bit impatient.

"All right, I'm coming . . . I'm coming."

Anna's fork falls to the floor. Father picks it up. "Look at that. Pieces of potato everywhere. You clean that up later, Anna!"

Anna places her hand over the telephone receiver and waits until her father has stopped grumbling.

"Hello," she says.

"Hello, this is Jet . . . Henriette Neumann. Would you please listen to me, Anna?"

"Yes."

"I wanted to tell you that I'm terribly sorry that I shouted at you so. Why didn't you tell me earlier that you were in hiding, too? And Anna, I promise never to talk about Max and Fannie when you come to visit me again. You will come, won't you?"

"Yes."

"Tomorrow?"

"I don't know."

"Don't be angry with me, Anna."

"I'm not."

Anna sets the telephone down. She has a cramp in her hand from holding it so tightly.

"Hurry up," her father says. "Your vegetables are getting cold."

Anna stirs her spinach with her fork. She doesn't feel like eating now. She must first think about her conversation with Mrs. Neumann.

"Come on, eat," says her mother. "Don't play with your food. Let's be glad that we have something to put on our plates again. Was that a girl from school on the telephone?"

Anna shakes her head.

"Who, then? A boy from school? No, that couldn't be. The name was Jet. That's short for Henriette."

"It was Mrs. Neumann," says Anna.

"Neumann?" Father sets his spoon down. "A German name?"

"Yes."

"Put your fork down. Give it here!" Father takes Anna's fork from her hand. "What's happening between you and this Mrs. Neumann? Something is going on, Anna. You're blushing."

"Give it back." Anna grabs her fork and begins to take large bites of her spinach.

"Who *is* she?" Father is very angry with Anna now.

"Mrs. Neumann is a woman who lives on the Vlietkade. I see her on my way to school and on my way home. She always waves to me. I know her name is Neumann because that's what it says on her door."

"Have you been inside her house?"

Anna is becoming terribly warm. She is beginning to sweat.

"Have you been inside her house?" Father asks for the second time.

"Uh . . . no."

"You're lying, Anna. You're red as a beet. I have just one thing to say: you are *not* going inside the home of a person whose name is Neumann. A German name! How dare you? Those rotten Nazis murdered our whole family!" Father slams his hand against the table. "My daughter has been visiting a Nazi!" he shouts.

"Calm down." Mother reaches out to stroke Father's head.

"Leave me alone!" he yells. "You're always trying to smooth things out."

"She won't go again," says Mother. "You won't visit that Nazi woman again, will you, Anna?"

Anna can't say anything more. How is she to tell her parents that Mrs. Neumann is Jewish, too? And that she is continually waiting for Fannie? If she told them that, they would cry again, just as they cried about Marga.

"I won't go anymore." Anna sighs.

"Good girl." Father tries to pull her onto his lap.

"Leave me alone," Anna snarls. "I'm going to bed."

◆ *Shoes*

"I'm keeping my gym shoes on," Anna says to Marion. "I'm going to have to run home."

"Are you having company?" Marion asks.

"No, I just have to run home, that's all." She doesn't want to have to explain to Marion that she must run past the white house and thus avoid Mrs. Neumann because she promised her parents not to see the woman again.

Anna puts her everyday shoes in her school bag.

"See you tomorrow!" Marion calls.

"Yes, see you tomorrow."

Anna walks slowly at first. When she is near the white house she will have to run very quickly past it.

She whistles to herself. The song they were singing before the bell rang is still going through her head:

How gently glides our little boat
O'er the sparkling lake . . .

The song is so soothing that Anna is becoming a bit sleepy. She chooses another song:

On the paths,
In the streets,
Forward march . . .

Anna is almost at the white house. She will do the same thing they do in gym class when they run: she will count to three. In gym class the teacher, Mr. Pauwels, does the counting, but Anna will have to count for herself now.

"One, two, three," she calls loudly. She begins to run. Just a little farther and she will be past the house.

"Stop, Anna!" Mrs. Neumann is standing in front of her with widespread arms. "You certainly are in a hurry. You're not going to disappoint me, are you?"

"I'm not going to disappoint you. I . . . I . . . my cat is having kittens."

"Your cat? Do you have a cat?"

"No."

"Well, then. I have something for you. Come, we'll go upstairs. We'll have a good time together. I'll make tea and I'll give you a piece of American chocolate. I've been looking forward to your visit so much. I've even gone out in order to prepare for it."

"All right." Anna sighs deeply. She can't refuse the invitation, for Mrs. Neumann looks so lonely.

A tea warmer is burning in the middle of the table. Anna pulls up a chair and sits down.

"Ready." Mrs. Neumann comes in with a teapot. "Delicious, real tea," she says. "How lucky we are to be drinking real tea again. Do you remember how that artificial tea tasted?"

"Of course I remember," Anna replies. "Mr. De Bree brought me tea in the afternoons. I would put my cup at one end of the table and pretend that there was a cup at the other end of the table, too. That other cup was for Kiki."

"Were there two of you? I thought that you were alone."

"I *was* alone. All alone in the attic room. I just pretended that Kiki was there. You couldn't really see her. I sang with Kiki and sometimes we played a game, checkers or Parcheesi. Usually Kiki won. And the whole time we played I could hear Mr. De Bree playing his trumpet downstairs."

Mrs. Neumann blows her nose. Her eyes have become red all of a sudden. Is she catching cold?

"Damn!" says Mrs. Neumann. "Damn!"

"Why are you swearing?"

"I'm angry."

"With me?"

"No, my dear. I'm not angry with you, I'm angry because of what happened *to* you."

"Oh, thank goodness."

"Can you play cards?" Mrs. Neumann asks.

"Yes, a little. The games I know are the ones that you can play by yourself."

"Would you like me to teach you some real card games? We are together now. You no longer have to play cards with Kiki."

Anna looks at the clock. It is already quarter past four! "I have to go," she says in alarm.

"Calm down," says Mrs. Neumann.

Anna rushes down the steps.

"See you tomorrow!" Mrs. Neumann calls.

"Surely you had to stay after school," says her mother when Anna is standing in the living room.

"Yes, I was having a lot of trouble with history."

"Surely you had to find out who the biggest liars in history were, didn't you?"

Anna stares at her mother. What does she mean?

"Why do you have your gym shoes on? Where are your regular shoes?"

"In my . . . oh, my school bag, I've forgotten my school bag."

"Would you like to know where your school bag is?"

Anna is becoming afraid of her mother.

"Your bag is with that German woman on the Vlietkade. I followed you and I saw you coming out of her house. Do you know who the biggest liar in history is?

You . . . you . . . you!" Mother pokes her finger at Anna's chest. Anna takes a step back.

"Away . . . out of my sight!" her mother shouts. "Go to your room and don't come out. Papa will bring you your supper and if he doesn't want to, then I'll do it. Now get out!"

Anna walks upstairs with her head bowed. Slowly she lies down on her bed. She can't stop crying, but she cries quietly; she doesn't want to be heard.

The door opens, and Anna awakens with a start. A man with a tray is standing in her room.

"Here you are," says the man.

"Thank you, Mr. De Bree," Anna says.

"Enjoy your food," says the man.

"The same to you, Mr. De Bree."

"You called me Mr. De Bree!" Father shakes her. "You are no longer in hiding. You're home with your own mother and father. Look, Anna. You're being punished only because you fibbed." He raises her chin with his finger. "Why do you do that?"

"What . . . what do you mean?"

"Why do you lie so much? You don't have to do that anymore. When we were in hiding we had to lie, but it's absolutely wrong to lie now."

"I didn't lie. I only fibbed a little."

"Children who fib deserve to be punished, too. We have to try to be a regular family again. You must stay in your room until we call you. I'm going downstairs. Enjoy your food."

"Don't think I'm going to eat!" Anna calls after him. "I'm not going to take a single bite!"

◆ In Hiding Again

More than an hour has passed, and no one has been upstairs. Anna is still lying on her bed. She hears her parents' voices downstairs. They are laughing. Music is playing . . . trumpet music.

The radio is turned even louder. Anna sits up. She hears music of Haydn, the same music she used to hear at Mr. De Bree's house.

"Run away, Anna," Kiki says. "Just run away."

Anna tiptoes down the stairs. Her parents' voices are mingled together and are louder now. Anna sneaks outside. She will run away to Mrs. Neumann's house. She never wants to come home again, for her mother and father are always angry with her.

Anna rings the doorbell many times in quick succession. It's a long time before Mrs. Neumann lets her in. She sets Anna down in a chair.

"Child," she says, "what's the matter? You've been crying."

"I was punished, so I ran away. They made me go into hiding again and I heard music of Haydn. My father was Mr. De Bree. I never want to go home again. I'll stay with you."

"Calm down, calm down," Mrs. Neumann whispers. "Get away, Amalia, Anna must get hold of herself first. Calm down, Anna. I'll get you a glass of water."

Anna's teeth are chattering so much that she can hardly drink.

"I'll help you," says Mrs. Neumann. She puts her hand under Anna's chin. "I used to do that for Fannie, too, when she was very small."

"I'm never going home again. Never."

"You shouldn't say that, Anna. It's a very big adjustment for your father and mother to have you living with them again. They've gone through a lot themselves, I'm sure. Do you know where they were when you were in hiding at Mr. De Bree's house?"

"No, they haven't told me, and *that* is what is so awful. They treat me as if I were a little child. They don't tell me anything at all."

"Maybe they can't talk about it yet."

"They can, too."

"Your glass is empty, Anna. Just this once I'm going to do something that I really shouldn't. I'm going to walk you part of the way home. I don't want your parents to worry about you."

"They won't miss me, anyway."

"Of course they'll miss you. I'll bet that they are already looking for you."

"I don't care. I don't care at all."

"Come on. I'll take you home."

Anna shuffles down the street, taking small steps as she goes.

"Not so slow," says Mrs. Neumann. "You know that I can't be away for long." She gives Anna a push.

Anna begins to move a little faster.

"I'll walk you to the tobacconist's shop, then I'm going back. Do you promise that you'll go straight home?" Mrs. Neumann asks.

Anna nods silently.

"Promise?" Mrs. Neumann says again.

"Promise," Anna replies.

"Goodbye, dear Anna. Go on. It's already getting dark."

When Anna is close to home she can see that the light in her room is burning. Anna is puzzled, for she didn't leave it on. Through an open window she hears her parents talking.

"I'll go. You'll just get all wound up," her mother says.

"And if she's not there? If she hasn't gone to that Nazi woman? What do we do then?" Anna can tell that her father is worried.

"She'll be there. I've already looked up her address in

the telephone book. On Wednesday we received a telephone book. We're in it, too."

"Judith, Judith, if only I knew more about bringing up
children. It's been such a long time since we've done it."

"You can do it, Simon, you can do it. Who taught
Anna to shout? *You* did. Don't you remember? We must
be patient."

Her father answers, but Anna can't understand what
he is saying.

She waits in the garden. Her parents are silent now.
She will go inside and tell them that she is back. Anna
opens the kitchen door and walks through the corridor.
She goes up the stairs, and opens her bedroom door. Her
room is empty! She looks in the bathroom. She runs to
her parents' room, then checks the rest of the house. No
one is home!

Trembling, Anna curls up in a chair. She hears the
snapping of a twig, and knows that someone must be
walking outside. She can hear heels clicking. Or are they
boots? She crawls into another chair. She hears footsteps
. . . by the kitchen window.

A telephone book on the floor is open to the letter N.
Anna would like to call Mrs. Neumann and ask her to
come take her back to her house, but she doesn't dare
leave her chair.

"Anna!" Her father and mother are in the room.

"Where were you?" Anna shouts.

"At Mrs. Neumann's house. We thought you were there."

"No, I mean where were you when I was in hiding at Mr. De Bree's house?"

Father sits down in a chair across from Anna. He crouches forward and cradles his head in his hands. "I can't talk about it," he says. "I just can't talk about it yet. Later, perhaps. I have to think about the future now, not about the past."

Mother sits down on the arm of the chair and strokes Father's head. "Anna," she says, "we now understand why you like going to Mrs. Neumann's house so much. We also know that she is not a bad German. Why didn't you tell us that she is Jewish, too, that she was in hiding, and that you've already told each other a lot about the war?"

"I didn't dare. I was afraid of making you unhappy. You never talk about the war with me."

"Keep talking," says her father softly. "Keep talking with Mrs. Neumann. I won't be jealous. I can't talk about the war yet. I'm a worthless fellow who can only deal out punishment. Are you still angry about your punishment? We have to get used to each other again, Anna. I have an idea. Ask Mrs. Neumann if she would like to come visit us sometime. Would you like that?"

"Mrs. Neumann can't leave her house," Anna replies, "and she always wears the same dress, the black one with blue flowers. Mrs. Neumann must wait for Fannie."

"Fannie? Who is Fannie?" her father asks.

"I'd rather not talk about it," Anna says. "We have to think about the future now, not the past."

✦ Girls, Bah!

Anna doesn't want to go to school today. She has a stomachache.

"I'm staying in bed," she says when her mother asks why she has not come downstairs. "I have a stomachache."

"Come on, Anna, don't be such a sissy."

"I'm *not* a sissy. I have a stomachache."

"Get dressed, Anna. Hurry up, you're already late. Do you know what I'll do? I'll write Mr. Pauwels a note excusing you from gym because of your stomachache. Would that be all right?"

"Mr. Pauwels doesn't pay any attention to notes from home," Anna complains. "Vera had a note from her mother once. She had a sore throat, but Mr. Pauwels made her take gym, anyway."

"You won't have to," her mother promises. "I'll write a nice note and I'll put it in a light-blue envelope."

"All right." Anna sighs. She wanted to spend the entire day reading in bed.

• • •

"All the girls in one long line!" Mr. Pauwels calls. "Vera, you stand in front since you're the smallest, and Anna, you stand at the end. The other girls can line up in between them."

Anna remains seated on the bench at the side of the gym.

"Come on, Anna," says Mr. Pauwels.

"I have a note, sir. I'll go get it."

Anna runs to the dressing room. She takes the blue envelope out of her school bag and returns to the gym.

"Here it is, Mr. Pauwels," she says.

Mr. Pauwels pulls the envelope out of her hand. "Do you know what I'm going to do with this?" he asks, glaring angrily at Anna.

"No, sir."

"Look." He begins to tear up the envelope.

"Don't, Mr. Pauwels!" Anna tries to stop him, but it is too late; the envelope is already in pieces.

"I'll bet you have a stomachache, don't you?"

Anna nods.

"That's what I thought. Girls and stomachaches, bah. What do you think, girl . . . all those women in the war . . . in the munitions factories. The women who had to take the places of men, because those brave fellows had to fight. Do you think that those women could go to their bosses with letters that said they couldn't work because they had stomachaches? You take gym, Anna!"

"No!"

"No? Are you sure? Then get out. There is the door. Into the corridor with you!" Mr. Pauwels points to the door. "Hurry up!"

Anna walks slowly through the gym. Slowly she opens the door and then slams it shut behind her. She is so angry that she can hardly breathe.

That Pauwels . . . talking about the munitions factories. The German munitions factories, of course. That man sided with the Germans during the war. He was wrong. Absolutely wrong. Anna doesn't want to stay in the corridor for a single minute. She doesn't want to be so close to someone who was a member of the N.S.B., the Dutch Nazi Party.

She fetches her school bag from the dressing room and walks down the long corridor. If she should meet a teacher, she will say that she is going home; that she must report Mr. Pauwels to the authorities.

Anna doesn't meet anyone. She walks out of school.

"I don't care if Mr. Pauwels worries about where I am," she says out loud. "It would serve him right. The dirty N.S.B.-er."

✦ Don Pedro

Anna bites down on her pen holder. These rotten sums! What difference does it make if Mr. B. has a garden measuring thirty square meters, or that Mr. C. walks from Amsterdam to Haarlem? Anna was in hiding when the other children began doing these arithmetic problems, so it's no wonder that she doesn't understand how to do them very well.

Anna sees the classroom door opening. Mr. Van Vliet, the sixth-grade teacher, enters with a guitar under his arm. He whispers to Miss De Wit, and they laugh together.

"Put your pens down," says Miss De Wit. "Mr. Van Vliet has something to tell you."

The class becomes noisy as all the children begin to talk at the same time. What is Mr. Van Vliet going to tell them?

"Would you listen for a moment?" Mr. Van Vliet asks. "You know that in a couple of weeks we are going to hold a big festival at school to celebrate our liberation. I'm doing a play with the sixth graders, and I'd like very much to do something with you, too. I'm looking for a girl who would like to play a Gypsy. She will sing a song, and I will accompany her on my guitar. First I'll let you hear the song, then whoever wants to be the Gypsy must raise her hand. If more than one girl wants the part, Miss De Wit and I will have to choose. Here is the song." Mr. Van Vliet strums a few measures and then begins to sing:

Pepita, with rings in your ears,
Pepita, with your soft brown skin,
Pepita, I want you to be mine,
Pepita, sweet Gypsy girl,
You'll be my bride, my kin.

Anna nods at Mr. Van Vliet. How handsome he is when he sings! His clear blue eyes are half closed. He continues:

I wish to dance the czardas with you,
I wish to kiss you in the night,
You are still too small, Pepita,
But Gypsy girls grow fast,
I'll wait for you.

Jan raises his hand.

"Yes, Jan?" says Mr. Van Vliet in surprise. "Do *you* want to be the Gypsy girl?"

"No!" Jan quickly puts his hand down. "I just wanted to ask if you wrote the song yourself."

"Yes," Mr. Van Vliet answers. "I wrote the words and the music, too."

"It's nice," says Jan.

The children begin to talk again.

"Quiet!" Mr. Van Vliet calls. "You haven't heard the Gypsy girl's answer yet, and it's the best part:

> Don Pedro, I wish to be yours alone,
> Don Pedro, it's true that I am small,
> Olives I'll eat, and paella,
> So that I will soon grow tall.

"Who wants to be the Gypsy girl?"

Anna raises her hand. Mr. Van Vliet takes a piece of paper and writes down ANNA MARKUS.

"Who else? DORINE VAN DIJK? Fine. BIANCA DANIELS. All right. Is that all? Going once, going twice . . . sold! Three ladies then. Come see me later. I'll give you the words and the music, and you can practice at home. Goodbye, Miss De Wit. Goodbye, children." Mr. Van Vliet walks out of the classroom.

Anna is standing in front of the mirror. Mama said that she could take anything she needed out of her closet. Anna has found a black skirt with gold flowers embroidered on it. A red blouse is hanging in the closet, too. She puts it on. That one bare shoulder really appears Gypsy-like. She will put on sandals, as well, and a pair of gold earrings . . .

Mr. Van Vliet is going to choose her. She has the darkest hair of anyone in the class. It was terrible to be brunette during the war. The Germans didn't like children who were brunette, but it's quite all right to have dark hair now.

"Anna," Mr. Van Vliet will say to her solemnly. "Anna, you have been chosen. You look splendid and you sing beautifully. Much better than those other two children." He will whisper that he let Dorine and Bianca try out for the part even though he had already chosen her. "Don't tell anyone, Anna," he will say softly. "This is a little secret between you and me." He will look at her with his velvety-blue eyes and kneel before her when he sings.

Mr. Van Vliet comes into the classroom. "You first, Anna," he says. Is he winking at her? Mr. Van Vliet begins to sing. How beautiful it sounds! Even more beautiful than yesterday.

Anna sings her part and dances a bit, a Gypsy dance.

"Thank you, Anna," says Mr. Van Vliet when she has finished. "Take your seat. Bianca, your turn."

Mr. Van Vliet sings for Bianca. How idiotic Bianca looks! She has a sort of nightgown on.

Anna sits comfortably at her desk. She knows for sure that she will be chosen. Just listen to Bianca! She is singing out of tune.

"Thank you, Bianca," says Mr. Van Vliet. "That was nice. Take your seat."

After all the girls have sung, Mr. Van Vliet and Miss De Wit go out into the hall.

"You've got the part," Lukas says to Bianca.

Anna bursts out laughing. That Lukas . . . he's crazy!

Miss De Wit and Mr. Van Vliet return to the classroom. The class is silent. Mr. Van Vliet begins to cough.

"The part of Pepita," he announces formally. "The part of Pepita goes to . . ."

Anna stands up next to her desk.

"Bianca Daniels!"

Anna sinks back into her chair. Bianca Daniels . . . ridiculous. She can't even sing and her hair is so blond it's almost white! Who ever saw a blond Gypsy?

Mr. Van Vliet . . . what a horrible man he is. He has the ugliest eyes she has ever seen; ugly, watery-blue eyes.

Don Pedro . . . what a phony!

✦ Hello, Saint Nicholas

"I'd like to tell you more about Fannie. May I, Anna? Would that be all right with you?"

"Yes," says Anna.

Mrs. Neumann begins:

"When we first went into hiding, Fannie wasn't with us. We hadn't seen one another for a long time, and you can understand that I missed her terribly. Max and I were living in the Mozartlaan, at the home of Koos Liebrechts and his wife. We didn't know where Fannie had been taken; that was for the best, for we couldn't betray her to the Germans if we were captured.

"I no longer felt like doing anything. I didn't read . . . I hardly talked. The only thing I wanted was to have Fannie with me.

"It was the end of November 1943, when Koos told me that he would try to come up with something; perhaps it was possible for us to have a chance to see Fannie.

"'I think I've got an idea. Be patient and wait,' said Koos."

"Well, did he have an idea?" Anna is so curious that she can't help asking.

"He certainly did. I'll tell you about it." Mrs. Neumann sighs deeply. She continues:

"It was about six o'clock in the evening on December the fifth, the birthday of Saint Nicholas, when Koos came upstairs. He set a large box down on the table. He told us to open the box and put on the clothes that were inside. Max opened the box. He looked in and then stepped back. 'No!' he called.

"I looked in the box, too, and you know what I saw, don't you? A Black Peter outfit and a Saint Nicholas costume! I asked Koos if it was his idea for us to dress up. He said that I understood the plan correctly. And so, disguised as Saint Nicholas and his helper, Black Peter, we would go with Koos to see Fannie, and no one would have the slightest idea who we were.

" 'How happy Fannie will be!' I called, and I was so thrilled that I began to dance.

" 'Stop!' said Koos. 'Stop!'

"I stopped dancing.

" 'You musn't tell Fannie who you are. You must promise me that you won't tell, otherwise we can't go. The people she is with don't want you to come. They think it's too dangerous.'

"I must have looked very disappointed, for Koos said that he could understand how difficult it was for us, but this was the only way to see Fannie.

"We began to get dressed. Koos and I couldn't help laughing at Max. What a splendid Saint Nicholas he was! I thought I looked good in my Black Peter costume, too. Koos darkened my face with a sort of shoe polish, and he told me not to sweat too much, because the black might run.

"We walked awkwardly down the stairs. Max almost tripped over his long robe. Suddenly we were standing outside. The cold felt wonderful, but we didn't have much time to enjoy the fresh air, for Koos pushed us into the car.

"How nervous we were! Max and I sat in the back seat, holding each other stiffly. He wore white gloves, I wore black ones.

"We came to a street where we had never been before. 'Fannie is at number three,' said Koos.

"We stepped out of the car. I was so nervous that I felt sick to my stomach, and I saw that Max was very white. Or had Koos painted his face that white?

"Koos rang the bell. A man who called himself Gerard opened the door. He told us to come in, and said that he was honored to be allowed to greet Saint Nicholas and Pete. He also informed us that he had invited some of his family for the occasion. 'Nieces and nephews and so on . . .'

"We were led into a room. We saw people sitting in a circle, grown-ups and children. I looked at the circle and I saw Fannie. Gerard brought us to a decorated chair. 'This is your throne, Saint Nicholas,' he said.

"Max sat down and I stood behind him. I looked at Max to see if he had noticed Fannie, too.

"The children began to sing, 'Welcome today in our midst.' Fannie's mouth was wide open, and I could see that she was already beginning to lose her baby teeth. 'You see your throne is ready,' she sang. I wanted to run to her and call that I was her mama and that she must come with me. Of course I didn't do anything; I stood erect behind Max's throne.

"Gerard gave Max a book with a large golden cross upon it. 'You left this book in the car, Saint Nicholas,' he said. 'And Pete forgot the sack of gifts.'

"I said that I felt like a pretty stupid Pete. The children began to yell and to boo. I started to dance a little, for I thought that a Black Peter should dance. I went up to a boy and asked if he could sing a song. 'Happy Birthday, Saint Nicholas,' he sang.

"Then I went over to Fannie and asked her what her name was. I wanted to know if she had been given a different name. She looked at me with her big brown eyes, but didn't answer.

"Max called me back. 'We're going to give Pete a spanking,' he said. 'Pete isn't doing his best today.' He turned me over his knee and spanked me with my own rod. The children shouted and clapped their hands. When Max was finished, I began to pass out candy.

"'Look,' said a girl, 'Pete cried. His cheeks are all streaked. Saint Nicholas must have hit him hard!'

"Then Max read from the thick book. 'Janneke Klaverman,' he called. A little girl approached. Max gave her a red knit doll and said that she had been very good during the entire year.

"A boy about eight years old was next. He received a car made from a cigar box.

"'Ria Groen,' called Saint Nicholas. Fannie came forward. So she *had* been given a different name!

"'I have a coloring book for you,' said Max, 'and I've heard that you are a very sweet girl. Would you like to give Saint Nicholas a kiss?'

"She kissed him on his beard. Then she came to me. I bent down to give her a handful of candy and whispered, 'Hello, darling.'

"And what happened after that, Anna . . . I could cry just thinking about it.

"'Hello, Mama,' she whispered. 'I want to go with you.'

"Fannie came to live with us in the Mozartlaan shortly afterward."

✦ Mask

"Didn't you ever go downstairs when you were at Mr. De Bree's house? I can hardly believe it. How could you stand being all by yourself like that?" Mrs. Neumann asks.

"I was downstairs once, and then another time, too."

"Do you want to tell me about it, Anna?"

"Yes, but it's a weird story."

Mrs. Neumann laughs. "Silly girl, with your weird stories," she says.

Anna begins:

"One day Mr. De Bree came upstairs without his serving tray. I thought it was strange, for he had never done that before. He sat down on my bed and said that he needed me. He was going to hold a recital of all his students, and he wanted a girl to dance to the music. He wanted _me_ to be that girl. I said that I didn't want to because it was much too dangerous. Mr. De Bree began to laugh as if he knew something that I didn't. 'I've thought of a plan,' he said.

"I asked what he meant.

"'I'll buy a mask for you,' he said. 'An angel's mask. You'll wear a white dress, and you'll have a kerchief on your head so that the audience can't see your black hair. You'll dance to the beautiful trumpet music.'

"I was so frightened that I was speechless. Mr. De Bree

said that I shouldn't be afraid because no one would see my face. 'No one will know who you are,' he said. He also told me to pay careful attention to him, because he would give me a signal when I could go back upstairs. 'At the very end of the piece I'll cough loudly, and then you can return to the attic. At least in this way you'll have been downstairs once.'

"I began to cry, and Mr. De Bree said that I shouldn't have such a poor attitude. He said that he had seen me dancing when he had brought me my meal a few minutes early one time. 'You were dancing like an angel,' he said.

"I wanted to tell him again that I was afraid and that I couldn't dance if my legs were shaking, but I couldn't say anything more; he had already gone back downstairs."

"Well, did you dance?" Mrs. Neumann draws her chair a bit closer to Anna.

"Yes, I had to. Mr. De Bree got me a rubber mask and a shiny, white silk kerchief. I put the kerchief on my head, and Mr. De Bree put the mask on my face. He held a mirror in front of me, and I couldn't believe I was that crazy angel. Mr. De Bree also brought a package containing a white dress. I had to put it on. I didn't have any shoes. 'When it's over, you can go upstairs more quietly if you're barefoot,' he explained.

"Mr. De Bree then began to whistle a song, something by Haydn, I think. I had to dance. The kerchief slid off my head. He said that he would fasten the kerchief tighter for the recital. 'You'll have wings for the performance, too,' he said, 'and remember, don't fly out the window!'"

"And then? Did everything go well?" Mrs. Neumann puts her arm around Anna.

"No, not at all." Anna shivers as she thinks about it. "Shall I keep going?"

"Of course. I'm listening."

"Well, and then there was the performance. We sat on long benches downstairs. There were a lot of children and fathers and mothers. The button on the kerchief hurt me under my chin, but I didn't dare loosen it. I was also terrified that the elastic band on the mask would break. I didn't want anyone to see my hair or my face.

"A little girl was sitting next to me. She kept trying to pull my wings, and I told her she mustn't do that.

" 'Kees, there's a little brat behind that mask,' a woman said to her husband.

"I wanted to tell Kees that I wasn't a brat, that I was only very frightened, but of course I didn't dare say anything.

"The younger children played first. Then an older boy had to play. Mr. De Bree gave me a push. 'Your turn, angel,' he whispered. 'Do your best.'

"The boy played, and I began to dance. It wasn't going very well. I was so hot with that mask on.

" 'Who is that adorable angel?' I heard someone ask.

" 'Another student, I think,' was the answer.

"Then my dancing began to go much better. It was as if I had real wings. I danced close to an open window, and I felt the wind on my feet and my hands.

"Then . . . suddenly . . . everyone began to clap. I had

to go back upstairs. I hadn't been paying attention to Mr. De Bree; he had probably coughed ten times, but I hadn't heard him.

"I started to run. I don't know how it happened, but I fell at full length in front of the people in the first row.

"I felt someone pulling on my mask. I felt my face coming into view. The little girl who had been sitting next to me was pulling on the nose of the mask. She stretched the elastic band and then let the mask snap back. It hurt. I pushed her, and she fell. I ran up the steps.

"'Miserable brat!' I heard someone call behind me. 'How dare you bully little children and then run away?'

"The woman had a shrill voice, and she was shouting so loudly that I could hear her all the way up in the attic room.

"'See, Kees, what did I tell you? A horrible brat is hidden behind that mask. She ran upstairs. Bah, what a cowardly angel. Come back, if you dare . . .'

"I lay down on my bed. I put my head under my pillow and I shouted as loud as I could. I shouted that I didn't want to be in hiding any longer, that everyone was mean to me, and much more. I shouted and shouted even though no one was supposed to hear me."

"Come," Mrs. Neumann whispers in Anna's ear. "Come close to me and shout now. Shout all you want. I'll hear you."

✦ *Fire!*

"The tea warmer keeps going out. I must ask my neighbor to buy me a new one." Mrs. Neumann is trying to light the tea warmer. Anna sees a small flame appear, but it lasts for only a moment.

"I'll try one more time. If it doesn't work, we'll just have to drink our tea cold." Mrs. Neumann strikes a match. She holds it at an angle in order to bring it close to the wick.

"Ouch!" she calls out. "Darn!" Mrs. Neumann drops the burning match on the floor.

"Fire!" Anna shouts. "Fire, I can smell it!" She would like to run to the kitchen to fetch some water, but she feels as if the chair has grabbed hold of her. "Fire!" she screams again.

Mrs. Neumann pours the tea from the teapot onto the floor and puts the flame out. "Stop screaming, Anna. What's the matter with you? Why the panic? There isn't any fire. It was just a tiny flame, and it's out now. I put it out. Why are you behaving this way?"

"I . . . I've been in a fire."

"In the attic room?"

"Yes, and I almost got burned. It was my own fault."

"My goodness, how awful. Do you want to tell me about it?"

"Yes . . . yes, I do.

"Mr. De Bree had brought my meal to me and he stayed longer than usual. That was because his cigar kept going out. He complained that these wartime cigars were getting worse and worse. He also told me to hurry up because a student was coming in a few minutes. He took a small box of matches out of his pocket and lit the cigar. Then he went back downstairs, leaving the box of matches with me.

"It was a pretty box. There was a little bird on it. The bird was flying through the air, and the air was yellow. I opened the box and started to play with the matches. I made figures: squares, triangles, crosses, and a Star of David, too, but I quickly destroyed that star.

"I struck a match. It was fun to watch the flame. I struck another one, and another. I blew the flame out each time. Then I wanted to see how long I could hold a burning match in my hand. I could do it for a long time. The flame came almost to my fingers. I could feel the heat."

"Aha," Mrs. Neumann says. "I'm beginning to have a better understanding of your reaction. Keep going."

"Well, and then I dropped the match on the floor. That's what I thought I did, at least. But the burning match landed right on the match box, and all at once a huge flame jumped up at me.

"I started to scream. I wanted to run to Mr. De Bree, but I couldn't. I heard music downstairs; the student had already come. I couldn't leave, and the fire had reached the chair I had been sitting on. Then I did something crazy. I ran downstairs and went outside, just like that. Out the door.

" 'Fire!' I screamed. 'Fire!'

"I wanted to go back into the house; it was so light outside. I pulled on the bell, but no one came. I rang the bell again and again. Finally Mr. De Bree opened the door, and he looked at me as if he had seen a ghost.

" 'Anna, what are you doing outside? Are you crazy?' He dragged me into the house.

" 'Fire!' I shouted. 'Up in the attic!'

"Mr. De Bree pushed me into a room. A student was standing there with a trumpet in his hands.

" 'A neighbor!' Mr. De Bree shouted. 'This girl is a neighbor. Take care of her. There is a fire upstairs!'

"The boy sat down in a chair. He looked at me. 'Where have I seen you before?' he asked.

"I didn't know what to say. I was so afraid that he knew me, therefore I kept screaming, 'Fire, fire!'

"The boy didn't say anything more; he shrugged his shoulders and began reading the newspaper.

"After a while Mr. De Bree came downstairs. He had black soot all over his face, and his clothes were soaking wet. 'Thank you for telling me about the fire, young neighbor,' he said. 'You can go home now. I'll see you to the door.'

" 'Goodbye, loudmouth,' the boy said to me, but I

didn't answer. 'All she did was scream,' he explained to Mr. De Bree.

"Mr. De Bree pretended to let me out, but he pushed me to the steps instead. He told me to go upstairs and not to be frightened.

"I *was* frightened. Everything was filthy, and there were puddles on the floor. It stank like smoked sausage. In the middle of the room was an upside-down bucket; I no longer had a chair. I sat down on my bed.

"Then Mr. De Bree came up. He had me drink some tea. It tasted bitter. He said that he had put something in it, something to settle my nerves.

"'Good grief, what a mess,' he said. 'Do you have any idea how the fire started?'

"When I said that I had no idea, Mr. De Bree looked at me. 'The matches,' he said, 'I left the matches here.'

"Then I began to scream that it was all my fault and that I was sorry that the whole place hadn't burned up; that I was sorry *I* hadn't burned up, because if I had, I would be just a pile of ashes and would no longer have to be in hiding.

"Mr. De Bree appeared to be very shocked. He said that I must never again say things like that — wishing that I were a pile of ashes — and now I understand why."

Mrs. Neumann nods silently.

"Mr. De Bree promised to clean everything up, and he promised that I would get a new chair. He sat down next to me and put his arm around me. He said that I must do my best to bear everything, and that my parents wouldn't be happy with a pile of ashes. I couldn't help laughing then. He asked if I would like for him to come upstairs and play the trumpet for me that evening. I said . . ."

"Well, did he? Did he play?" Mrs. Neumann asks.

"I think he did, but I'm not sure."

"How strange. Why aren't you sure?"

"I had to drink the bitter tea all up, and I became so drowsy from it that I fell asleep. I think I slept until the following afternoon."

"I'm going to make some fresh tea," says Mrs. Neumann. "Delicious tea without bitter tranquilizers. Although *I* could use a tranquilizer after hearing your story."

"Not really?" Anna says. "You don't really need a tranquilizer, do you, Mrs. Neumann?"

"Maybe just a little." She kisses Anna's hand. "My dear sleepyhead, don't you worry about me."

◆ *Pain*

"It was terrible that Fannie and Max were caught while I was gone, wasn't it?"

Anna is just about to roll the dice on the Parcheesi board.

"Will you please listen, Anna? I *must* tell you about it.

Today would be Max's birthday. That's why I can't help thinking about our last day together."

The dice fall on the table.

"All right," Anna says with a sigh. "Tell me." She is curious, yet at the same time she finds it eerie to learn the reason that Mrs. Neumann is alive today.

Mrs. Neumann begins her story:

"I had a terrible toothache. I hadn't slept for a week. We had tried everything: pills, and we had put the last of Koos's gin on my tooth. Nothing helped.

"'You can't go on like this, Erika,' Koos said to me. 'We'll have to do something about it.'

"'That's easy for *you* to say,' I told Koos. 'You can go anywhere you want, but what am I to do? I could be caught, and you know what that means. The concentration camps at Westerbork . . . Poland . . .'

"'Don't worry, Erika,' Koos said, trying to soothe me. 'Listen. I know a dentist who is good, a man who won't betray you. Don't ask me how I know, just trust me. I'm going to call him and say that Mrs. Erika van Waardenberg is coming. I'll be very careful. I won't tell him everything, but he'll understand. Don't worry. You'll have to go by yourself because that will be safer.'

"I looked at Max.

"'Go on,' Max said. 'Go. Something must be done about your tooth.'

"'Okay, I'm going to call him now.' Koos ran downstairs. In five minutes he was back.

"'You can go,' he said. 'Right now. And remember,

walk normally. Don't look nervously around you. Just act the way you used to act when you went to the dentist.'

"I can still hear Max's laughter. 'Well, well,' he said to Koos, 'I see that you don't know what she used to be like when she had to go to the dentist. She was one big bundle of nerves. I had to think of all sorts of ways to calm her down, and even then I practically had to drag her to the dentist.'

"Koos laughed, too. 'Put your coat on and go,' he said.

"I put on my winter coat, the same one that I wear now. I put my hat on. I kissed Fannie and Max, not knowing that this would be the last kiss Max would ever receive from me.

"I saw myself in a long mirror that was hanging in the hall. A strange person looked back at me, a strange person with long, unkempt hair. How long had it been since I'd seen the hairdresser? I saw a white face surrounded by the gold frame of the mirror. The stranger had a swollen cheek, and a little red hat was perched at an angle on her head.

"'I'm going!' I called.

"'For God's sake, be careful.' Max came into the hall to give me a final kiss.

"'Goodbye, Mama!' called Fannie.

"I stood outside in the cold. It was winter, the twentieth or twenty-first of January. I can't remember what the exact date was. I felt the wind on my aching cheek; the pain was becoming even worse.

"I heard the sound of my heels on the cobblestones, a sound I hadn't heard in a long time. I began to tiptoe.

" 'Don't, Jet,' I said to myself. 'Ordinary people don't walk on tiptoe when they're outside.'

"I went to the Olafstraat, the street that Koos had directed me to. The address was number fifty-five.

"I didn't have to ring the doorbell. I was expected. A man in a white jacket let me in. 'Come, Mrs. van Waardenberg,' he said. 'Take off your coat.' He led me to a room that smelled like Lysol. 'Please sit down,' he said.

"The dentist put a sort of bib on me. 'Otherwise I'll spoil your lovely flowered dress,' he said. 'Open your mouth, please.'

"I did everything he asked, and the crazy thing was, I wasn't frightened. I was so happy that I had arrived safely.

" 'This one must come out.' The dentist tapped a metal instrument on my aching tooth.

" 'Pull it. I don't care,' I said.

"I was there for half an hour. Then I was standing outside again. I walked back calmly. Everything had gone well. There was not a Nazi to be seen. My mouth was numb from the anesthetic. If it hadn't been, I think I would have begun whistling a tune. I was so relieved!

"I was almost at the Mozartlaan when I felt a hand on my shoulder.

" 'Don't go any farther,' someone said. 'Quick, come with me!'

"A man was pulling on my sleeve. I tried to get loose.

64

" 'Don't go any farther, I tell you,' he hissed. 'There is a roundup. The Nazis are inside . . . at Koos Liebrechts's house.'

" 'Fannie!' I screamed. 'Max!'

"I was pulled into a house. 'Stay here!' The man shouted even louder than I. 'You're safe. I'm Hans. I've seen you before, at Koos's house.' He put his hand over my mouth. 'Be quiet, otherwise I'll have to hit you, and I'll hit you hard, too!'

"There was nothing more to be done. I *was* quiet and I remained quiet. For days . . . weeks. It was as if my mouth stayed anesthetized all that time. Max and Fannie were caught, and I wasn't . . .

"The next day Hans took me to another address. Somewhere in Friesland and . . ."

Mrs. Neumann stops and looks at Anna. "Good God, what have I done?" she whispers. "I won't talk about Fannie and Max anymore. Go on and roll, Anna. Where are the dice? Do you want some punch?"

Anna drinks her punch in small sips. Mrs. Neumann is drinking tea.

"How cozy it is together, Anna," she says. "It's a bit like a birthday, isn't it? I'm drinking tea and you're drinking festive orange punch."

Anna accidentally tips over her glass.

"Do you want me to refill it?" Mrs. Neumann asks.

"No . . . no more festive orange punch for me," Anna says.

◆ Oh, Glorious Colors

"Children," Miss De Wit says, "I have an invitation for everyone in the fifth and sixth grades. The mayor has decided to present a choral concert in tribute to our liberation. We have a couple of weeks to practice. First we'll rehearse at our own school; if that goes well, we'll practice in a large auditorium with children from all the schools of the city. If *that* goes well, we will sing in the church square. Perhaps Queen Wilhelmina will come listen. We'll be singing patriotic songs. Who knows some?"

Pieter raises his hand. " 'Holland, They Say!' " he calls.

Miss De Wit looks at the piece of paper in her hand. "It's on the list," she says. "What other songs?"

" 'Oh, Glorious Colors.' "

" 'Where the White Tops of the Dunes . . .' "

All the children are shouting at once.

"Enough . . . enough!" Miss De Wit puts her hands over her ears. "You realize that these are all songs that we weren't allowed to sing during the war," she says. "I know that there were people who were shot for singing them. Nearby. At the . . ."

Anna is startled. She doesn't want to hear any more talk about dead people. She doesn't want to think about them anymore. She has already thought *so* much about them. About Marga . . . about Grandpa and Grandma.

Anna wants to be like all the other children who don't think about dead people.

". . . that we're beginning tomorrow." Miss De Wit said something, but Anna didn't hear it.

"We'll continue with Switzerland," the teacher says. "Get out your atlases."

"The source of the Rhine River is in Switzerland. It rises in the Alps," recite the children in a singsong manner.

Anna sighs. Switzerland . . . there was no war in Switzerland. If only Anna had lived there! She wouldn't have had to go into hiding then.

"One, two, three. We begin on the fourth count, children." Miss De Wit has a baton in her hand. She taps it against her desk. "Pom, pom, pom, pom," she sings.

"Oh, glorious colors
Of Holland's flag,
How proudly you wave
By the tide . . ."

sing the children.

Anna finds it splendid. She doesn't know how it happens, but she is getting goose bumps all over her body. She gets them whenever she feels that something is beautiful. She thinks that she has goose bumps now because she is hearing a song she knows people died for if they were caught singing it. If only Miss De Wit hadn't told them about it. But perhaps she *had* to talk about it for the ordinary children who don't know as much as Anna does.

They sing all the songs, and Miss De Wit is very satisfied. "I want our school to be the best," she says. "I'd be pleased if the mayor and the queen said that our school was the most musical one in the whole city."

After much practicing, it is time for the schools to rehearse together. All the children have gathered in a big auditorium.

A large man carrying a strange sort of instrument is standing on the podium.

"That is the conductor, and he is holding a megaphone," Miss De Wit explains. "Otherwise it would be impossible for all five hundred children to hear him."

"Quiet!" calls the conductor. "Quiet, we're going to begin. First we'll sing 'Oh, Glorious Colors.' One, two, three!"

They sing the song in two-part harmony, and it sounds wonderful. Yet even though the children make very few mistakes, the conductor interrupts them.

"Stop!" he calls. "Stop! I need to know something important. Are there children present who suffered extra during the war? No, I don't mean this past winter, the Hunger Winter. That was very bad, because thousands of people starved to death. But what I mean is this: are there children here who were in a concentration camp?

Or children who were in hiding, or in the resistance?"

Anna feels herself turning bright red. Here they go again. Everyone is looking at her. Even the conductor is looking in her direction.

"Who, then?" he asks.

"Anna, sir. Anna was in hiding for a long, long time!"

"Rotten Martijn," Anna calls.

"And Bart delivered newspapers. Illegal newspapers!" shouts Emma.

"Anna and Bart, come to the podium," calls the conductor through the megaphone. "Everyone must be able to see you, and if our queen comes, you'll surely be allowed to shake her hand. Good, Bart is already here. Now Anna."

Anna remains in her place. She doesn't want to come to the podium. She wants to stand with the other children. The conductor can go to hell with his patriotic songs.

"Come on!" says the conductor. "I can't see you among all the other children. Where are you, Anna?"

Anna stands at her place with her mouth tightly closed. She doesn't move.

"Take it or leave it!" calls the conductor impatiently. "Come, now, children, sing! One, two, three . . ."

"Oh, Glorious Colors . . ." sing the other children.

◆ Photo

Anna stands dead still by her desk and stares at a small white vase filled with poppies. Those flowers weren't there when she left for school this morning; the water spots on the brown wood weren't there, either.

There is something else on her desk, as well: two eyes are peeking out at Anna from behind the flowers. Photo eyes. Who has set that picture frame there, with the photograph of Marga? Who has startled her so?

Anna sits down on the bed and puts her hand over her eyes. With her other hand she gropes for a handkerchief, but she can't find one.

"Well, Anna, what do you think?" Anna didn't hear anyone come in, yet suddenly her mother is sitting on the bed.

"But it's not allowed, is it?" she says a bit angrily. "Papa can't stand to see photos of murdered people, can he? He said so himself a couple of weeks ago. When I was so unhappy about Marga."

"It's all right," her mother replies, and she strokes Anna's hand. "We talk a lot, Papa and I. You don't notice, but we talk a lot. About everything that happened to us. And Papa said that he didn't think it was fair to forbid you to keep a photograph of Marga in your own room. He wanted to tell you so himself, but I wanted to surprise you. We won't set out any photos downstairs, for the time being. Maybe we will someday. It all happened such a short time ago. Your father doesn't know that Marga's picture is already up in your room."

"There'd have to be many photos downstairs, wouldn't there?" Anna whispers.

"Yes, I'm afraid so." Her mother sighs and begins to count on her fingers. "Jetty, Marcel, Fieke, Leonard, Theo . . ."

"Stop," says Anna. "You would have to use the fingers on your other hand and then you wouldn't have enough. If *all* of us counted on our fingers, we still wouldn't have enough."

Mama presses Anna against her. "Gone," she says. "Murdered . . . just like that . . . because they were Jews. But *you* are still here. Sometimes for no reason at all, Papa and I say to each other: 'Anna is still here.' "

"Fannie is, too," says Anna, and she is startled by her own remark; she doesn't know why she said it. "Never mind," she adds.

"Mrs. Neumann is still waiting, is she?" her mother asks. "Maybe she should quit waiting. That's no life. Always alone in that big house and always wearing that same dress."

"Her dress is almost completely worn out," Anna says. "There's a big tear under the arm, but she won't wear any other dress. Only that black one with the blue flowers."

"Bring it home sometime," says her mother. "Then I'll

see if I can mend it. But she will have to wash it first. When you're standing close to her you can smell that she hasn't washed it in a long time."

"You're mean." Anna is becoming angry at her mother. "Mrs. Neumann doesn't smell bad. I know that she washes her dress often. 'When you're standing close to her,' you said. Have *you* ever stood close to her?"

"Of course, Anna. Don't you remember that you ran away and that we looked for you? We were on the Vliet-kade then, in her house. No, that's not completely true. *I* was in her house. Papa stayed outside. Later, when we were walking home, I told him everything. Anna, I'm having a difficult time with your father. Maybe I don't pay enough attention to you, for I have the feeling that I'm always having to protect him. He has suffered so much."

"And you haven't?" Anna asks.

"Yes, I have, too."

"I hear Papa." Her mother walks to the hallway. "We're upstairs, Simon," she calls.

The outside door closes with a thud. "I'm coming, I'm coming!" her father answers.

What is Anna to do? The photo . . . her father doesn't know about it yet. She tries to snatch the picture, but she misses and knocks over the little white vase. Water spills on her desk. Before the photo becomes wet she grabs it and hides it under the bed covers.

"Anna and I have been sitting together on her bed and having a cozy visit," Anna hears her mother say. "I'm going back up to her in a little while."

"I'll go now," she hears her father say.

Anna dries her desk with a handkerchief and sets the vase with the poppies upright again. Then she sits down on her bed, very carefully. Imagine what would happen if she sat on Marga's photograph. The glass could break. She can't bear to think about it.

"Hello, Anna, here I am," her father says, and he starts to sit down on her bed.

"No!" she cries. "You go sit in my chair."

"But your mother . . . she said that you were both sitting on your bed. Don't you think that I'd like to sit on your bed, too?" Father looks terribly hurt.

"Anna won't let me sit next to her," he tells Mother when she has joined them. "Now that I want to talk with Anna, she doesn't want to."

"I do want to talk, but I don't want you to sit on my bed," Anna says. She notices that her mother is looking at the desk.

"Anna, where is the . . ."

Anna dives under her covers and remains there in the darkness.

"Here!" she cries when she reappears. "Here is Marga's photo. She's dead. Everybody is dead these days!" She lays the picture down on the covers.

Father stands next to Anna, completely motionless. With wide eyes he looks at the photo. "Did you hide it because of me?" he whispers. "Did you hide Marga's picture under the covers so I wouldn't see it? Is that why you didn't want me sitting on the bed?"

Anna nods.

Father sits down in Anna's chair. "Sweetheart," he says softly. "You don't have to do that anymore. I really am doing my best to bear everything. I'm fighting against myself. One day you won't have to hide anything from me. No photograph and no experience. No experiences of yours or of anyone else, either. And one day I'll be able to tell you what happened to your mother and me when you were in hiding at Mr. De Bree's house."

Anna climbs off her bed and sits in her father's lap. He holds her stiffly in his arms.

"Shall we agree to that?" he asks.

"Agreed," Anna replies.

"Get off my lap," her father says, and he gives her a little push. He walks to Anna's bed and picks up the picture.

"Set it down," he says. "I think that Marga's picture was on your desk. By the water spots and by the flowers. Oh, those poppies . . . how sad they look." Father peers into the vase. "No water," he says. "They have no water. Give them water, Anna. Otherwise they'll die. We must have living flowers next to our photos. Beautiful, living flowers."

✦ We'll Meet Again

> We'll meet again,
> Don't know where,
> Don't know when . . .

Every Wednesday afternoon the street organ plays new songs. Songs that were written in England and in the United States during the war.

Anna has heard the songs so often on the radio that she can sing the words, English words that may now be sung again.

The melodies are played by the most beautiful organ that Anna has ever seen. Standing on the outside of it are four dolls that sometimes play the triangles or drums. Occasionally the dolls move their heads. They look so real that Anna feels like nodding back to them.

Anna spends every Wednesday afternoon outside, for she doesn't want to miss the street organ. She enjoys watching the organ grinder, too. He turns a wheel with a large, sweeping motion of his arm. When he turns it slowly, the music is slow; when he turns it fast, the music gets faster, too.

Sometimes the organ grinder becomes so hot that he must wipe his head with a big red handkerchief. He does that between songs. Anna doesn't understand why he always has such a heavy sweater on. He wears a navy-blue sweater even on warm days.

Anna isn't certain, but she thinks that the organ grinder likes her. He looks at her in such a nice way, and he has winked at her, too. Last week he even asked her what song she wanted to hear. There were many children dancing around the organ, but he had asked *her*.

"I want to hear 'Vivian Loves a Canadian,'" Anna replied. "That's a Dutch song and I can understand it, at least."

"Silly girl," said the organ grinder. "Music you understand always, whether it's sung in English or Dutch."

He played the melody, and Anna sang the words. When she was about to put money into the copper cup, he looked at her. "I won't take any money from you," he said.

Anna doesn't understand why he accepted money from all the other children, but not from her. Today she will try again to put money into the cup; he *must* take her money this time.

Anna wipes her face on a corner of her red skirt. How hot it is today! The asphalt is practically melting on the street. She hopes that there will be a thunderstorm this evening and that it will cool off, for this kind of heat is unbearable. She sits down on the fence. The organ grinder will be along soon. There are other children waiting for him, too.

"In this hand I have pennies for the organ grinder,"

says a little girl. "I'm allowed to put a whole lot of money into the cup."

"I have money, too," says Anna. "I wasn't allowed to give him money last week."

"Oh, I was. There he is. I hear him." The child begins to dance. "The organ is coming! The organ is coming!" she calls.

"We'll meet again . . ." The tune is coming from the end of the street. The sound becomes louder . . . louder.

The organ is finally in front of Anna and the other children.

The organ grinder wipes his head. "Hot, isn't it?" he calls. "I left my sweater at home." He begins to turn the wheel. The dolls join in playing the music, too. Sweat is pouring down his face. "I can hardly stand it!" he says. "Aren't you hot, children?" He begins to roll up his shirt sleeves.

"Keep turning! Keep turning!" a boy shouts.

"Let me roll up my other sleeve first. I'm nearly suffocating!" After he has rolled up both sleeves, he begins to turn the wheel again.

"Vivian loves a Canadian . . ." Anna sings the words loudly. "Vivian loves . . ."

She looks at the man's bare arm. A number . . . he has a blue number on his arm, just like Aunt Floor. Aunt Floor was in a concentration camp, in Auschwitz. The Nazis tattooed a number on her arm there.

Then the organ grinder was also . . .

The music stops. The organ grinder turns and walks toward the children.

"Why aren't you singing?" he asks Anna. "I was playing the song just for you."

"The number . . . the number on your arm."

The organ grinder looks at his arm. "Oh, that," he says. "I don't pay much attention to it anymore, but now that you know, I can tell you."

"What can you tell me?"

"That I met a nice girl in Auschwitz, a girl who looks very much like you. That's why I don't want to take your money. That's why I play songs for you. That girl . . . the same eyes. The same birthmark on her forehead."

"What is her name?" Anna speaks so softly that she can barely hear the question herself. She hardly dares to ask it.

"Her name was . . . her name was . . ." The organ grinder taps his hand against his forehead.

"Keep turning. Keep turning, organ grinder!" shout the other children.

"I forget her name," he says. "My memory fails me every now and then."

"Fannie . . . we're trying to find Fannie Neumann. I look like her."

"Yes, that was her name. Fannie Neumann."

Anna grabs his arm. "Where is she?" she shouts. "She has to go home to her mother."

"Ow, you're hurting me. Look what you're doing to my arm." He pushes Anna's hand away.

"No, that wasn't it. Her name was Ilja, not Fannie." He wipes his forehead again. "What difference does her name make, anyway? She's dead. She died at the end of January, a few days before we were liberated. Come on, I have to get back to work. I have to put food on the table. What would you like me to play, my dear? Wait, I know. Listen."

"We'll Meet Again," plays the organ.

"You like this song, don't you?" he calls.

"No, I don't like it. I don't like it one little bit."

"Don't be angry with me," says the organ grinder, and he sighs. "I didn't start this damned war. This dirty, rotten, stinking war.

"Goodbye, my sweet girl. See you next Wednesday. If the good Lord is willing, we'll meet again next Wednesday."

A melody can be heard at the other end of the street: "Vivian Loves a Canadian."

✦ Stupid Heroes

"Today I want to tell you how I ended up in hiding at Mr. De Bree's house, but it's not a very happy story."

"That doesn't matter," says Mrs. Neumann. "It couldn't possibly be a happy story. War isn't happy."

Anna begins:

"One day Papa and Mama asked me to come into bed with them. They had something to tell me. I crawled in between them and asked what it was. They told me that someone was coming to pick me up. I was going into hiding. Of course I didn't know what going into hiding was.

"Mama said that she would take the yellow Star of David off my clothes so that no one would know I was Jewish. The man picking me up would take me to a house where a man and a woman and their three children lived. The next day my parents would be there, too.

"I asked what the children's names were, but my mother didn't know. She didn't know where the house was, either.

"The doorbell rang that afternoon. Papa opened the door for a man who called himself Jeroen. Of course that wasn't his real name. Jeroen asked me to come with him. I wanted to. I gave my parents a whole lot of kisses and I went with Jeroen. He promised that I would see my father and mother the next day.

"We walked a long way, and finally came to a forest. We went in. Jeroen stood by a thick tree. He said that he was going to leave me by that tree and that in ten minutes someone else would come to fetch me.

"I asked Jeroen what that person looked like. Jeroen said that it would be a man wearing a blue raincoat and a white scarf.

" 'The man will say "Hello, Maria" to you,' Jeroen said.

"I told him that my name was Anna, not Maria, but Jeroen didn't hear me. He had already left, and he waved to me in the distance.

"I was all alone in the forest. At first I didn't think it was so bad. I thought that the man in the blue raincoat would come soon, but he didn't. It was taking a very, very long time, and I was becoming frightened. I didn't know what time it was, but I was sure that ten minutes had passed long ago. I didn't dare stand under the tree because I was afraid that a branch would fall on my head. I walked to a path and stood there.

"I had to go to the bathroom, but I didn't dare. If the man came while I was doing it, he would see my bare bottom, and I didn't want that! I was also afraid that a wolf would come. I heard dogs barking in the distance. Bloodhounds, I thought.

"All of a sudden someone next to me said: 'Hello, Maria.' I looked up and saw a man with a cigar in his mouth. He wasn't wearing a raincoat or a white scarf, either. He said that I had to go with him because Jan, the man who was supposed to have come, had something else to do.

"I didn't say anything at all. I was afraid that this man was a traitor. When he said that he was in the resistance, I went with him. I couldn't stay all by myself in the forest, could I? He said that we were going to his house, and that I was a brave girl because I had been alone in the forest for more than an hour.

"I asked what the names of his children were. He didn't answer, so I asked him again.

"'Children?' he said. 'I don't have any children. I don't even have a wife.'

"I didn't understand it at all. I was supposed to be going to a home that had three children. I said it was mean; that my parents had lied to me. He looked at me, then said: 'I'll tell you the truth. That plan has fallen through. The man who was supposed to have come here to fetch you has been caught.'

"I began to cry, but the man wouldn't let me. He said that I must be brave. I asked when my father and mother would come.

"'You'll hear about it,' he said. 'In any case, you're coming with me now.'

"I began to cry again, and the man said I should be grateful. Grateful because he had received a signal from the underground informing him that a Jewish child had been left behind in the woods. Otherwise who knows when I would have been found?

"We had to walk a long, long way. Finally we came to a house. A sign that read DANIEL DE BREE, TRUMPETER was on the door.

"I was taken upstairs, to the attic room. And I stayed there all that time. Alone, and . . ."

Anna stops and looks at Mrs. Neumann. Has Mrs. Neumann had that angry expression on her face for long?

"I'm sorry," says Anna. "I didn't mean to make you angry."

"Those stupid idiots!" shouts Mrs. Neumann. "They should know better than to leave a little child alone in the woods, even if they *are* in the underground!"

"People in the underground are heroes," Anna whispers.

"Yes, perhaps." Mrs. Neumann can't help laughing a bit. "Stupid heroes exist too, Anna."

✦ Train

Anna has thought about it for a long time. Actually she doesn't dare go, but she wants very much to make Mrs. Neumann happy. Who knows, perhaps she will find Fannie among the children in the train that will be arriving this afternoon.

Yesterday Anna read an article in the newspaper:

> A train carrying children who survived the concentration camps will be arriving tomorrow afternoon at the main station. The children, all of whose parents died in the camps, will be met by orphanage personnel. Arrival time has been set at 15:48 hours.

Anna calculated that 15:48 hours is approximately a quarter to four. It took her a while to figure it out, but she knows that is the correct time. A quarter to four. Anna can go to the station at a quarter to four. If she dares.

Anna *does* dare. She is on her way to the train station. She didn't tell anyone where she was going. Mama thinks that she is with Mrs. Neumann. Mrs. Neumann thinks that she is at home. If only they don't call each other on the telephone! But they never call each other. Why would they do so today?

Although such thoughts help to reassure her, they don't make her stomachache go away. Should she turn back? Perhaps those children will look pitiful. Perhaps they will be skin and bones, and will have been shaved bald because of the lice they had. Anna knows exactly how it was because Roosje told her all about it. Roosje returned from a camp, together with Father. She told Anna all about it, just once, and afterward the girls played as if nothing out of the ordinary had ever been discussed. After that one time they never talked about the camp again.

It is very busy at the station. Adults are coming and going, but no children are present. Anna looks at the clock and sees that it is already three-thirty. She feels sick; her stomachache has gotten worse, and the back of her neck is beginning to hurt, as well.

Two big men are standing next to her. "Sir, what do you know about the condition of these children?" one man asks the other.

"It's bad . . . awfully bad, my good colleague. They were totally malnourished when they were found. However, a few of them are in a somewhat better situation because they were liberated in January."

"It's a shame, sir, it's a shame that there are so few of them. You could call it a miracle that these children will soon be arriving. How did they manage to survive under such terrible circumstances? Even we doctors will not be able to do much for them. Let's hope that they will receive good attention from now on. They will have many problems to overcome."

Anna walks a bit farther up the platform. She doesn't want to listen to those two men. She knows that it is not too late to turn back.

Anna remains at the station.

She finally hears a train in the distance. She sees it, too; there are puffs of smoke hanging above the engine that is gradually approaching.

The train comes to a full stop. A woman steps out, a woman in a white coat. Anna sees her stretching her hand toward a child who is standing in the doorway. The nurse lifts the child from the train. It's a little girl.

Fannie?

Anna wants to run to the train, but she is held back. "A child," someone says. "What are *you* doing here? This is no place for children."

"I'm . . . I'm looking for my sister. She's on the train." Anna doesn't know what else to say.

"That's a different story," says the man. "Go on. Walk to the train."

Anna runs ahead. She is now right by the nurse, who is walking in front of a small line of children. No one says a word; Anna hears only the clacking of wooden shoes, which all the children are wearing.

A message is broadcast through a loudspeaker: "The children who have just arrived at platform nine are to report to the station restaurant with their caretakers. I repeat, the children who have just arrived at platform nine are to report to the station restaurant with their caretakers."

Anna walks to the restaurant. She stands against a wall. She will be able to get a good look at everyone now.

The children enter very quietly. They are thin and dressed in clothes that don't fit well. Hardly daring to move, they remain standing.

"Sit down," a nurse tells them.

Anna can barely hear the sound of the chairs being pulled out from the tables. She hears the children talking softly. Anna looks at them.

There, just a little way from her, is Fannie!

Anna approaches the child. "Are you Fannie?" she asks.

The little girl looks at Anna silently.

"His name isn't Fannie. His name is Thomas," says a boy.

Anna is becoming depressed. She can't even tell the

boys from the girls. The children all look the same to her.

Over there . . . that child *must* be a girl. She has brown eyes, and she has a birthmark on her forehead. She probably used to have curly hair, too.

"Are you Fannie?"

"No," the little child whispers. "I don't think I'm Fannie."

Anna wants to leave.

"Did you find your sister?" asks the man who wanted to keep Anna from running to the train.

"No."

One little girl in the group doesn't want to stay in her seat. She dances through the restaurant.

"Would you look at that," says one of the doctors. "It's unbelievable. The little imp is indestructible."

"Why are you dancing?" he asks the child.

The little girl stands still. "We came in a pretty train," she says. "A real passenger train. When we went to the camp, we rode in a cattle car, and that's why I'm dancing."

"Damn," says the doctor. "How old are you?"

"Ten."

"Much too small, damn!"

Anna can't bear it at the station any longer. Fannie isn't here. She may as well leave.

"Perhaps your sister will be coming later," says a nurse. "Would you like a sandwich, just like the other children?"

"No, thank you," Anna replies.

Anna runs away. If she doesn't get home she is going to be sick.

Where is Fannie?

♦ *Russian*

Anna is having trouble sleeping. She still doesn't know what she is going to do for her teacher's birthday tomorrow.

The list that Johan has been keeping in his desk has a lot of names on it. Names of children who are going to do something unusual at the birthday party. Anna has seen the list.

I'M GOING TO STAND ON MY HEAD, Marion has written on it.

I'M GOING TO PULL A LIVE RABBIT FROM A HAT, Marcel wrote down.

I'M GOING TO PLAY THE RECORDER. I'M GOING TO BLOW A SOAP BUBBLE AS BIG AS A SOCCER BALL. I'M GOING TO . . .

Almost everybody is going to do something, but Anna still doesn't know what she is going to do. She can't do anything unusual. She can't stand on her head or perform magic tricks.

Anna turns over in bed and throws off her covers. She

has an idea! She will recite a poem, which she can do very well. She knows a wonderful poem; it's in the book that she always kept with her during the years she spent in hiding. The poem is in *The Book for Youth*, on page ninety-nine. Anna knows that poem from memory.

"Night is not angry . . . when the night comes . . ." She recites it to the end. The poem is so beautiful that it gives her goose bumps. But what if the other children don't like it? What if they talk while she is reciting it? And what if they laugh . . .

"I won't do it," Anna tells herself. "I just won't do anything."

Suddenly she sits up in bed. Why didn't she think of that in the first place? Of course . . . *that* is what she will do. She will write down on the list: I'M GOING TO TALK, ANNA.

She crawls back under the covers, laughing a little. "And now go to sleep, Anna," she says to herself.

"Anna is going to do something special," Johan sneers as he reads what she has put down on the list. "What's so great about talking? You do it every day! Even when it's not the teacher's birthday."

"Just wait," says Anna, and she tries to look secretive.

It is a wonderful celebration. Miss De Wit is wearing a party dress, a red one with a white ribbon under her collar.

"Happy birthday to you," the children sing. "Happy

birthday to you." Marion stands on her head, Marcel pulls a live rabbit out of a top hat. Ineke plays the recorder, and Jan blows soap bubbles. The children are growing noisier and noisier.

"Anna!" Johan calls. "Your turn. Let me announce you: ladies and gentlemen, we're going to listen to Anna. And what is Anna going to do? She's going to talk!"

"Talk?" Miss De Wit is surprised.

Pieter turns around in his chair. "Talk . . . what's so wonderful about that?" he grumbles.

Anna is already standing in front of the class.

"Quiet!" Johan yells.

"Doog gninrom, syob dna slrig," says Anna. "Ereh si Ssim Sukram."

"What's this, Anna?" Miss De Wit stands up next to her chair. "What language are you speaking?"

"Jewish!" shouts Kees.

"You mean Hebrew, don't you?" Miss De Wit says, and shakes her head. "No, Hebrew sounds different. I heard Hebrew spoken once, when I was visiting some Jewish people."

Anna doesn't say anything, but she laughs a little.

"Swedish!" Marion calls.

"Danish . . . Spanish . . ." All the children are shouting at once.

"I'll tell you!" Anna tries to shout above the others. "I'm speaking Russian! 'Good morning boys and girls, here is Miss Markus' is what I said."

"Russian, yes, that's what I thought," says Miss De Wit with a nod. "I think Russian is a splendid language. And in my opinion your pronunciation is excellent. Whom have you learned Russian from?"

"From . . . from Aunt Floor. Aunt Floor was liberated by the Russians in Auschwitz and then a Russian soldier fell in love with her and he came back to Holland with her. I have Russian lessons from him every day."

Anna is so carried away by her fantasizing that she can hardly stop. "And that Russian boyfriend of hers . . ."

"Do you know what, Anna?" says Miss De Wit, interrupting. "You know what? Yuri is in the sixth grade. He speaks Russian all the time with his father. I'll go get him. Then you can talk Russian to each other for the class. I think that would be very interesting."

Miss De Wit runs out of the room.

"Did you really learn that from a Russian?" Marcel asks.

"Quiet!" Anna shouts. "Please be quiet for a minute. What am I going to do? Soon she'll be back with Yuri and then I'll have to speak Russian and it's not Russian at all. I'll write it on the board."

Doog gninrom . . . Anna takes the pointer and directs it to the right of the first word, to the letter g.

"Read with me!" she calls.

"Good morning," the children read.

"I get it!" exclaims Vera. "Anna is speaking backwards. You can talk backwards to Yuri, Anna. Just tell him that you're speaking a different kind of Russian than he is. Russian from the Ukraine, or something."

"It's a shame . . . a shame . . ." says Miss De Wit as she returns to the classroom. "Yuri is sick, Anna. We'll try again another time."

The children are laughing so hard that they are hanging over their desks.

"That's nice," says Miss De Wit sarcastically. "That's nice of you to laugh when you hear that a child is sick. Anna, next week, perhaps. I'm sure Yuri will be better by then."

"I epoh ton," Anna replies. "Ssim Ed Tiw, esaelp, I epoh ton!"

✦ A Fountain Pen

"Come upstairs quickly, Anna. I have something for you, something nice."

Mrs. Neumann can hardly wait for Anna to get upstairs. Anna is still downstairs in the hallway. Mrs. Neumann has just opened the door for her.

Anna is very curious. What does Mrs. Neumann want to give her? It must be a gift, of course!

"Here it is." Mrs. Neumann places a package on the table in front of Anna. It is wrapped in flowered paper and topped with a large, purple bow.

"Go on, Anna. Open it. It's for you."

Anna carefully begins to unwrap the package.

"Tear it," says Mrs. Neumann. "Otherwise it will take forever. I can't wait any longer."

"The paper is so pretty. It would be a shame to tear it."

Finally, Anna has unwrapped the package. A small, narrow box is resting in her hand.

"Do you have any idea what it is?" Mrs. Neumann asks.

Anna does have an idea. She thinks that it is a fountain pen, a red one, but it would sound too greedy to say so.

"Well, what do you think?"

"A . . . a fountain . . . a letter opener."

"No, it's much more valuable than a letter opener."

"A . . . a fountain pen."

"Wrong. More valuable."

"A watch?"

"No."

Anna has run out of guesses. Why doesn't Mrs. Neumann just give the present to her? Why does she have to make it so complicated?

"Open it."

Anna removes the lid from the box. She sees a wad of pink cotton inside.

"Keep looking," says Mrs. Neumann, and she laughs.

Anna pokes her fingers underneath the cotton. She feels something, something hard. She removes a layer of the wadding.

Underneath, on another layer of cotton, is a key.

"Take it," says Mrs. Neumann.

"A key?" Anna doesn't know what to think. It is an ordinary metal key, just like the keys that her parents have. There are letters on it, but the key isn't made of gold or silver; why does Mrs. Neumann say that it is so valuable?

"You don't know what to do with this gift, do you?"

"I . . . I've never had a house key before," Anna stutters. "And whose house is it to, anyway?"

"Anna, silly Anna. Whose house do you think? Think very hard, now."

"I *am* thinking. I'm thinking as hard as I can."

"Here is the answer: the key is to *this* house, to Henriette Neumann's house."

"Oh, but you always open the door for me, don't you? I . . . I'm afraid I'll lose it."

"I'll take some string and crochet a chain for you. If you put the key on the chain and wear it around your neck, you can't lose it."

"No chain, please. I'll put the key in my school bag."

"You aren't happy with the key, are you?"

Anna doesn't reply. Why is Mrs. Neumann looking so earnestly at her?

"Anna, I never would have given you my key if I didn't love you so much."

"Oh . . ."

"You must promise me something. From now on, let yourself in with this key. Don't ring the doorbell anymore."

"No, I won't ring the bell anymore." Anna sighs. "But you musn't be angry if I forget. If I ring the doorbell, anyway."

"I won't be angry. The idea is that someone will be coming in, just as it used to happen years ago. I heard the sound of the key in the lock whenever Max came home, and I would be so happy then. One day you'll understand how valuable such a key is."

"Fine," says Anna. "One day."

"Say, Anna . . ."

"*Now* what do you want?" Anna nearly blurts out, but she stops herself just in time. She is still angry about the fountain pen.

"Did you look in the box carefully? Under the last wad, too?" Mrs. Neumann picks up the box and gives it back to Anna. "Look again."

Suddenly Anna feels very happy. Could there be a fountain pen inside, after all? She lifts up the last wad of cotton and finds a rolled-up piece of paper.

"Yes, that's what I mean." Mrs. Neumann smiles.

Anna unrolls the paper.

"Read it," says Mrs. Neumann.

Anna must hold the paper open with both hands to keep it from rolling up again. "Tickets, good for two admissions to the Draaikolk," she reads.

"Well, Anna, how do you like it? My neighbor went to

the Draaikolk and bought them at the cashier's office there. With my money, of course. Ouch, you're crushing me!" Mrs. Neumann pretends to avoid Anna's embraces. "Ow, stop, Anna. My dress . . . it's already so torn. That was approximately thirty-four kisses." They laugh together.

"It's nicer than a key, don't you think, Anna?"

"Yes . . . no . . . a key is nice, too. I'll use it all the time. I won't ring the doorbell again. I'll just come up the steps."

"Good . . . good. And if I were you I would save one ticket for a week from Wednesday. The biggest swing in Holland will be unveiled then. My neighbor said that forty people can ride on it at the same time. It's called 'the family swing.'"

"I'm going to watch the puppet show twenty times. It's because of the puppet show that I gave you so many kisses."

"Aren't you going to ride on the family swing or on the merry-go-round?"

"I don't know yet. I'll see."

"You should play, Anna . . . play. During the war . . ."

"Shhh." Anna puts her hand over Mrs. Neumann's mouth. "Please, no war today," she says. "Let's laugh again, just as we did when I gave you thirty-four kisses."

◆ Reading Aloud

Anna doesn't want to talk to Otto Oudoorn. She thinks that he is a horrible boy. Before she went into hiding he always called her names. At that time Otto was two years behind Anna in school, but they are in the same class now.

Otto used to sing a song whenever he saw Anna wearing a big yellow star that the Germans forced Jews to display on all their clothes. Anna can't get that song out of her head. It went like this:

> Stars on their blouses,
> Stars on their coat,
> We'll drown all the Jews
> In a great big moat.

Otto would then sing "Splash, splash," as loudly as he could.

Sometimes Anna feels like tripping Otto, or spitting in his face. She hasn't tried to do anything, however, because he is so big and heavy. Anna thinks it is a shame that she has never been able to get even with him.

Something pleasant is happening today. Miss De Wit must be away for an hour, and she has put Anna in charge of the class in her absence.

"You're in charge because you are the oldest," Miss De Wit said. "Have them work on their language lessons. If they misbehave, write their names down on the board. When I get back I'll think up a nice punishment for them."

She gave Anna a fresh piece of chalk, then left. Anna is determined not to write any names on the board; she doesn't want to be a tattletale. She has no desire to be that, but she does think it will be fun to play teacher for a while.

"I'm going to read to you," she tells the children. Anna can read aloud very well. While she was in hiding she read aloud to Kiki all the time.

Anna reads her favorite fairy tale of all, "The Little Match Girl." She knows it practically by heart. How fortunate that it is lying right on Miss De Wit's table!

It is dead still in the class. When Anna has finished reading, the children become a bit noisy.

"What a sappy story," says Jos. "And what a stupid girl she was to go barefoot in the snow like that. It was probably twenty below zero!"

"And now she's dead . . . dead . . . dead!" Otto pretends to sob.

"Read another story, Anna!" calls Noortje.

"Once upon a time . . ." Anna begins.

"Oh, no, not another fairy tale," Vera complains.

"Once upon a time there was . . . a little girl," Anna continues. "The girl was Jewish, and she was persecuted by the Nazis. She was no longer allowed to do anything. She wasn't allowed to swim or to go to a park, she wasn't allowed to attend school with non-Jewish children, and she could go shopping only between three and five o'clock. Of course the stores were sold out of all the good things by then. And so in various ways the Nazis tried to torment the girl."

"I'll bet this story is about you," says Pieter.

Anna doesn't reply. "One day the girl had to wear a big yellow star on her coat and on her dress," she continues. "In the middle of the star was the word 'Jew' written in large, phony Hebrew letters, and the girl thought that *that* was the very worst thing of all. If she forgot to wear the star, the Nazis would have sent her to a concentration camp and killed her there. Therefore the girl never forgot to wear the star.

"A very unpleasant little boy lived near the girl. He always called her names. Whenever he saw her, he sang a song that went like this:

> Stars on their blouses,
> Stars on their coat,
> We'll drown all the Jews
> In a great big moat.
> Splash . . . splash.

Anna stops talking. She looks at Otto and sees that he has become very pale. He ducks down and pretends to get something out of his desk. No one in the class says a word.

"And naturally you want to know who that mean little boy was, don't you?" Anna says very loudly.

"Yes . . . yes!" call the children.

"I'll give you a hint. He's in our class, and his name is spelled the same way backward as it is forward." Anna sticks her tongue out at Otto.

Otto slinks out of his seat. "I have to go to the bathroom," he says.

"Go on," says Anna, "but be quick about it."

"Otto!" calls Marcel. "It was Otto, of course. What a rotten kid!"

Anna picks up the chalk. "Take a good look," she tells the children. She begins to write. The chalk makes a screeching sound as it moves across the board.

> Otto, stupid Otto
> Had to go pee,
> And crazy Papa Oudoorn
> Is in the N.S.B.
> Splash . . . splash.

The children begin to laugh. "It serves him right!" Tineke giggles. "It serves him right. Here he comes."

Otto is standing in the class.

"Look at the board!" calls Tineke.

Otto stands still, then walks to the board and spits on it. He takes out a handkerchief and erases the poem.

"Funny poem, wasn't it, Otto?" Anna whispers. She must walk away to keep from slapping him.

All the children are in their seats when Miss De Wit returns.

"How nice and quiet it is here," she says. "No names written down, Anna? Fine. I'm glad that I was able to get away for a while. Make yourselves comfortable. I'll read aloud for a half hour or so. The story I'm going to read to you is 'The Little Match Girl.'"

◆ Bracelet

Anna tiptoes up the steps. She wants to surprise Mrs. Neumann. She is going to approach Mrs. Neumann very suddenly, put her hands over Mrs. Neumann's eyes, and call out, "Guess who!" Anna hopes that Mrs. Neumann will be sitting with her back to the door, otherwise her plan won't work.

The door to Mrs. Neumann's room is open. Anna tiptoes in. Mrs. Neumann is sitting with her back to the door. Why isn't she wearing her dress? Why is she sitting in her slip? Anna is so startled that she forgets about her plan.

Mrs. Neumann turns her head to look at Anna. "I

can't help it," she says. "I forgot that you could let yourself in with your key. Otherwise I would have wiped my eyes."

"What's the matter? Why aren't you wearing your dress, and why are you crying so?"

"See those pieces of paper on the floor?" Mrs. Neumann points to the wastebasket. Bits of torn paper are lying all around it. "That was a letter from the Red Cross. It said that they will no longer be searching for Fannie outside of Holland. Fannie never arrived at a camp. Not Bergen-Belsen, not Auschwitz . . . she didn't show up anywhere. Anna, I think she died in a train, on her way to a camp. What am I going to do now?" Mrs. Neumann begins to cry again.

"Keep looking," says Anna. "Keep looking. Fannie will be found. I know it for sure."

"How can you be so certain?"

"I know that Fannie will be found, but I don't know how I know."

"Where do you get your premonition?"

"From out of the blue, I think."

"Have you had it before?"

"What?"

"The feeling of knowing that something will be happening ahead of time."

"Yes, often."

"Oh, well," says Mrs. Neumann, and she sighs. "Adults can do it. Why shouldn't children be able to do it, too?"

"Fannie is coming back," says Anna. It doesn't matter

very much to her whether it is true or not; in any case, Mrs. Neumann doesn't look so unhappy now.

Anna bends down and picks up Mrs. Neumann's dress. "Here," she says. "Put it back on." Mrs. Neumann doesn't seem to hear her, yet she allows Anna to slip the dress over her head.

"Let me button it for you," says Anna.

Mrs. Neumann walks to the closet. When she is seated at the table again, she sets a small box down in front of Anna.

"Here, Anna. For you. You've seen it before. It's the silver coin bracelet. You wear it."

"No."

"Why not?"

"It's Fannie's."

"Fannie isn't coming back. Fannie is dead."

"Fannie *is* coming back!" Anna shouts. "No, don't take your dress off!"

Mrs. Neumann begins to cry again, loud, shrill cries. "Wear it," she sobs. "Give me that pleasure now."

"Fannie is coming back. Believe me!"

"Fine, fine. Then give it to Fannie when she comes . . . if you're right. Bring your arm closer."

Anna leans her elbow on the table. The clasp makes a clicking sound as Mrs. Neumann fastens the bracelet around her wrist. The cold feeling of the coins against her skin makes Anna shiver.

"Pretty," says Mrs. Neumann. "Wear it in good health."

"Not at all," Anna replies, "for I'll be giving it to Fannie soon."

"I hope so," Mrs. Neumann whispers. "I hope so. And if you're right . . . I don't dare think about it."

"But it's true," Anna says. "I *know* I'm right."

✦ Catching Butterflies

There is a new boy in the class. His name is Stefan. No one knows why he has just begun attending school here.

No one?

Anna has heard that he came to live with an aunt and an uncle because his parents are in prison. "Stefan's parents are N.S.B.-ers," she heard. "Stefan's father betrayed Jewish children."

Because of these rumors, Anna doesn't want to have anything to do with Stefan. She realizes that children can't help it if their parents have done cruel things, but it is quite possible that Stefan himself was in the children's N.S.B., in the Jeugdstorm. Members of that group wore black fur caps with orange trim, and they could sing and march just as well as the adult N.S.B.-ers could.

Everyone torments Stefan. Anna does, too. Stefan almost never does anything to fight back. Sometimes he spits at a child when the harassing becomes too much for him, but he never fights. He merely stands in the school-yard with his hands in his pockets. Anna thinks that Stefan becomes so angry from the teasing that he doesn't have hands in his pockets at all, but fists.

No one defends Stefan, not even Otto. Anna knows why Otto doesn't help him. Otto is naturally afraid that the other children will begin to bother *him* again. He has a bit of a respite when Stefan is around, for the children pay more attention to Stefan than they do to him.

Sometimes Anna "accidentally" hurts Stefan. Sometimes she steps on his toes. Stefan never does anything to fight back. He hasn't even spit on her. Once Anna laughed at Stefan, too, very loudly, when Kees suddenly held his arm out at an angle and called to him, "Heil Hitler!"

During the war Anna often heard members of the N.S.B. greet one another in this manner. "Drop dead," she would think to herself, whenever she heard it. She never did say it out loud, for that would have been much too dangerous. But it's not dangerous now, therefore she and Kees called to Stefan, "Drop dead."

Anna said it many times. She just couldn't help herself. "Drop dead . . . drop dead . . . drop dead . . ."

Anna still knows many German songs from memory. She sings one of them whenever Stefan is nearby: " 'Und wir fahren gegen Engeland . . .' " While marching through the streets, the German soldiers used to sing the song when they wanted to let people know that one day they would be marching through England, too.

Stefan doesn't do anything to Anna, even when she sings " 'Und wir fahren . . .' " He merely looks at her.

When Anna enters the schoolyard in the afternoon she sees a small group of children gathered around Marius, a sixth grader. He is holding a jar in his hand.

"Look," he says. "These two are Small Whites, and I'm not sure what the third one is. I don't know the names of all the butterflies, but I'll look it up at home."

"When will you let them go?" Marion asks.

"Let them go? I'm not letting them go. I'm going to drug them, and they'll die. Then I'll pin them by their wings onto a blue velvet board. I have over a thousand butterflies. They all have pins through their wings," Marius tells them.

"Step aside." Anna pushes her way through the circle of children.

She is now close to Marius, who is holding the jar above his head. The butterflies flutter against the jar, high above Anna.

"Give it here!" Anna stands on tiptoe. "Don't kill them." She is nearly in tears. "Let them go. It's mean!"

"I'll let them go if you give me three kisses. I want a kiss for each butterfly. Come on, Anna!" Marius stoops down. "Here . . . here is my mouth. Kiss me. Are you going to do it?"

"Anna doesn't kiss animal torturers," she hears someone say.

Anna turns to see who has spoken. Next to her, in the
middle of the circle, is Stefan.

"Listen to him talk!" Marius shouts. "Shut up, you
dirty N.S.B.-er!"

"Give it to me," says Stefan. "Give me that jar right
now, or I'll beat you up!"

"He'll beat me up! That dirty N.S.B.-er is going to
beat me up!" Holding the jar with one hand, Marius tries
to punch Stefan with his other hand. "Just because I've
caught three stupid butterflies . . . ow!"

The jar smashes against the pavement.

"Ow!" Marius shouts again. "That rotten Nazi . . . he
kicked me in the stomach!"

Anna feels someone holding her. She shakes her shoulder in order to get Stefan's hand off.

Stefan thrusts his hands into his pockets. He looks up
at the sky. "There they go, Anna," he says. "Look,
they're free . . . all three of them."

Anna doesn't know what to say.

"Well, how do you like that? How do you like being
helped by an N.S.B.-er?" He draws his face close to hers.
"Aren't you going to sing any more German songs for me?
'Und wir fahren,' maybe? Whose side are you on, Anna?"

"Go away," says Anna.

Marius is standing amid the broken glass. He raises his
arm in the Nazi salute. "Heil Hitler!" he shouts.

"Drop . . ." Anna puts her hand over her mouth. She almost called out, "Drop dead," but she doesn't want to do that anymore.

"Heil Hitler!" Marius calls again.

"Drop . . . drop . . . *alive!*" calls Anna.

✦ Fannie Is Coming

"Yoo hoo! Here I am, in the bathroom. Come in, Anna!"

Anna does as Mrs. Neumann asked, and enters the living room. It looks as though someone is having a birthday. The table, which is decked with a white cloth, has three cups, two cigars, and a platter of cookies on it. What is going on? Is Mrs. Neumann having company? How can that be? No one else ever comes to Mrs. Neumann's house, no one except the neighbor who does Mrs. Neumann's shopping. Anna is so surprised by the table that she forgets to sit down.

"Anna, Anna! Great news, great news. Sit down. I'm absolutely mad with joy!"

"What is it? What's happening? Tell me."

"Yesterday evening a friend of ours called, Frank van Berkel. He was with Max at Bergen-Belsen, and what he told me . . ." Mrs. Neumann can hardly continue. "He told me that Max arrived at the camp without Fannie. No, don't look so sad, Anna. Listen. When the Germans were inside the house on the Mozartlaan, Max had a chance to push Fannie out onto the balcony. Therefore she wasn't caught; she wasn't arrested. And now I have a little secret to tell you. You'll be able to see Fannie today. Wonderful, isn't it?"

Anna doesn't know what to do. Mrs. Neumann looks so strange. Her cheeks are red and her eyes are almost black. Perhaps she has a fever, and everything she said about Frank van Berkel is not true at all.

"Well, what do you think? Aren't you happy?"

"Yes, I'm happy, but . . ."

"Don't you believe me? Just wait. Soon you can see Fannie."

"Your dress . . . you have your ordinary dress on."

"Yes, of course. Why wouldn't I have it on?"

"But you were going to put the red dress on when Fannie came . . . and where did they find her?"

Mrs. Neumann waters the plants. "Don't ask," she says. "Be patient and wait."

"Shall I set Fannie's bracelet by her plate?" Anna inquires.

"By Fannie's plate? No . . . no, that's not necessary."

Anna doesn't understand a single thing that is happening. Mrs. Neumann laughs a bit, yet she looks unhappy. She is sitting at the table and staring straight ahead. She doesn't seem to notice Amalia rubbing against her legs.

She doesn't even notice when the cat jumps onto her lap.

"Mrs. Neumann," Anna says softly.

"Yes, what is it?" Mrs. Neumann whispers.

The doorbell rings. Why doesn't Mrs. Neumann hear it? Why doesn't she run downstairs and give Fannie a hundred thousand kisses?

"The doorbell, Mrs. Neumann." Anna begins to rise, but Mrs. Neumann pushes her back into her chair.

"I'll go," Mrs. Neumann says. The bell rings again. She walks slowly to the hall. Slowly she walks down the steps.

Anna hears a man's voice downstairs. Her heart is pounding in her chest. She is going to see Fannie now!

The voice becomes clearer. ". . . that I suddenly found you yesterday. That *you* are still here. Jet . . . Jet is still here."

There is the sound of footsteps on the stairs. Mr. De Bree's footsteps sounded exactly like that. Anna hears Mrs. Neumann's footsteps, too, but she doesn't hear a child's footsteps. Perhaps Fannie is being carried; perhaps she can no longer walk.

"Frank, this is Anna." Mrs. Neumann has flung the door open. "Anna, this is Frank van Berkel. I've already told you that he was with Max at Bergen-Belsen."

Mr. van Berkel offers Anna his hand, but she doesn't want to shake hands with him. She runs to the hallway. "Where is Fannie?" she calls. "Where did you leave her?"

"First a cup of coffee and a cigar," she hears the man say. "Is she always so wound up like this?"

"Why are you lying to me?" Anna is nearly in tears.

"I'm not lying to you," Mrs. Neumann replies.

"Shall we, then?" asks the man.

"Yes . . . yes, go ahead." Mrs. Neumann sighs.

"Do you have a white sheet, Jet? And can I set the case down here?" The man puts a black suitcase down in the middle of the table, next to the cookies.

Anna wants to leave. Perhaps they are going to wrap Fannie up in a sheet and then let her suddenly appear.

Mrs. Neumann returns with a sheet draped over her arm.

"Good," says the man. "We'll spread it across this wall. All those dresses have to come down." He begins to throw the American dresses into a heap. "Is this all right?" he asks, "or should they be neater?"

"That red dress should be neater," says Mrs. Neumann. "I have to wear it when Fannie comes."

Anna begins to shake all over. She wants to run away, but her legs won't let her. She remains in her chair, motionless. "Is Fannie downstairs?" she asks.

"Just wait," says the man, and he slaps the suitcase. "Fannie is in here."

Anna doesn't say a word.

"Do you think you can manage, Jet?" he asks.

Mrs. Neumann nods.

The man opens the suitcase. "Come look," he says to Anna.

Anna doesn't move.

Mrs. Neumann fetches a chair. "Set it on here. Wait, I'll help you." Together they bend over the case and lift a sort of camera out of it. "There is an electrical outlet." She points.

A light goes on inside the projector. "Close the curtains," says the man. "This movie projector doesn't give a very clear picture."

The room grows dark.

The sheet that the man has hung on the wall becomes very bright. Numbers dance overhead. Six . . . five . . . then . . . a little girl. Over her arm she has a shopping bag that is much too big for her.

A signboard: FRESH BREAD.

The little girl again. She is trying to climb up the brick steps.

In the bakery. The child stands on tiptoe and lays something down on the counter. Little hands put bread into the shopping bag.

The bakery steps again. The little girl walks carefully down, step by step.

"Look out, Fannie!" Mrs. Neumann shouts. It is too late. The child falls from the step. A woman comes running to her. She comforts the child and kisses her. The woman is pointing to Anna!

Anna looks. The woman who is looking right into the camera . . . that woman is Mrs. Neumann.

The child's head becomes larger. She is now looking at

Anna, too. Anna sees a birthmark on her forehead. A big tear runs down her cheek, then she begins to laugh.

An adorable little girl . . . curly hair . . . small white teeth . . . The wall becomes dark. Suddenly the room is so bright that Anna must shut her eyes.

"Nice, wasn't it, Anna? That was a nice movie. I wanted to surprise you. Do you see that you look just like Fannie?"

Anna is speechless. She feels just as she does at night when she has bad dreams, dreams about Marga or Grandpa and Grandma. She feels someone putting an arm around her and she hears Frank van Berkel's voice right by her ear.

"Really, we're going to find Fannie," she hears. "She must be somewhere in Holland. We're going to place a notice in all the Dutch newspapers, and ask who has seen Fannie. It's a miracle that Max was able to push her onto the balcony. If she had been captured, I never would have shown this movie to Jet and you."

Mrs. Neumann kneels before Anna. "Now you've seen Fannie," she says. "You've seen her now, Anna. Fine, isn't it?"

Anna does not dare say that she doesn't think it is fine at all, that it has only made her feel terribly sad. She sees that Mrs. Neumann is weeping. Mr. van Berkel has tears in his eyes, as well.

"Would you like to watch a cartoon?" he asks. "Charlie Chaplin or Popeye?"

"I don't know."

"Both, then," Mr. van Berkel decides. "Do you have time, Jet?"

"Oh, yes," Mrs. Neumann answers. "I have all the time in the world."

✦ Furniture and Books

Papa and Mama are talking a bit about what happened to them during the war. Anna is glad, for she feels that she can tell them more, too; about Fannie and Max and Mr. De Bree.

Her parents no longer worry so much about her. They are no longer so strict with her if she doesn't feel like eating at mealtime, for example.

Anna thinks that because her parents have relaxed a little, it is easier for her to fall asleep at night now. She doesn't brood so much. Sometimes she does feel sad, of course, especially when she thinks about all her friends who have died.

It is very cozy today. Mama has decked the table beautifully with a blue tablecloth and with two white candles.

"Anna may light the candles today," says her mother. "I'll do it next week."

Anna thinks it is nice to light candles on Friday evening. "We light the candles to greet the Sabbath," Mama explained. Anna had almost forgotten that Saturday was the Jewish Sunday, and that that Sunday actually began on Friday evening. It was very different when she was living at Mr. De Bree's house; one day was just like all the rest there. That is why Anna has forgotten a little about how it used to be, when she and her parents were at home together.

The spoons make a tinkling sound on the plates. The candles crackle softly.

"This is the nicest evening of the whole week," says Anna.

"I think it is, too," her father agrees.

Mama is silent.

"How quiet you are, Judith. Is something wrong?" Father lays his spoon down by his plate and looks earnestly at Mama.

"No . . . nothing bad." Mama laughs a little. "It's crazy," she says. "All of a sudden I began thinking about that white tablecloth with those pink flowers. Remember? I embroidered that tablecloth myself."

"It was a beautiful tablecloth," says Father. "I remember it."

"I've also been thinking about our piano and our bed. I can't help it."

"How did this come up?"

"I don't know, but it makes me feel so ashamed. We've lost so many people, yet I think about *things*. But I can't stand it that the Nazis took everything we treasured away from us. Everything . . . they took everything out of our house and sent it to Germany, just like that. Who knows, perhaps the painting of the Coolsingel is hanging on the wall of some Nazi's house. And my parents gave it to us with so much pleasure when we were married. A moving van pulled up in front of our door the day after we had gone into hiding. All of our possessions were loaded into it and driven directly to Germany. A woman who used to live near us told me about it herself. I saw her at the grocery store."

"Amalia might have kittens," says Anna. She tries to get her parents to talk about something else, but she can't; they keep talking about their plundered house. Anna wouldn't mind listening to such conversation on any other evening, but Friday evening should be cozy.

"What do you miss most of all, Anna?" her father asks.

"Marga."

"Of course you miss Marga, but that's not what I mean. I mean *things.*"

Anna doesn't need to reflect for long. "My books," she says.

"Oh, that's right." Mama's fork is poised in midair. "You made lovely blue jacket covers for all your books."

"Yes, and on each book I put a label with a number on it. Next to my bookcase I posted a list of titles with their numbers after them. I still remember some of the names: *My Name Is Theo* and *Kruimeltje* and *The Doppertjes.* For my tenth birthday, Grandpa and Grandma gave me a children's encyclopedia, and that's gone, too. Really now, those German children can't read Dutch, can they?"

"It's stupid that we get so worked up about things, isn't it?" her mother says. "I don't know why I'm like that."

"We don't get worked up about *things*." Father raises his voice. "We get worked up because for no reason at all, everything was taken away from us. Everything was stolen, and we couldn't do anything about it."

"Yes, everything from our former lives was stolen," her mother whispers. "We must start all over again."

"And we'll do it, too." Papa sits up very straight. "We'll show everyone that we're going to get on with our lives. What do you think, Anna?"

"Yes," Anna replies. "We're going to get on with our lives. Shall we get on with celebrating Friday evening first?"

Her parents laugh. "Silly Anna," says her father. "Do you know what we're going to do? When I have time, we'll go to the bookstore and buy you a whole pile of books. As for you, Judith, I'm going to get you a new tablecloth to embroider. A tablecloth with pink flowers, Judith."

Anna is too excited to remain in her seat. She gets up from the table and kisses her father soundly on both cheeks. "When are we going?" she asks.

"I said when I had time, didn't I?"

"Come," says Mama. "Let's continue our Sabbath celebration."

"*Sheer hama'alot beshu Adonai . . .*" In Hebrew they sing Psalm 126.

"Friday evening is fun, isn't it?" says Anna.

✦ Alone in the World

Papa always tries to keep his promises. He can't always keep them, of course, because something could come up in the meantime, but he never breaks a promise if he can help it.

That is why he and Anna are on their way to the bookstore together. They don't have far to walk. Anna enjoys going out with her father. It makes her feel as if things are a bit as they used to be years ago, before the war.

A man in a blue suit approaches them. He peers at them through his gold-rimmed glasses. "How can I be of service to you?" he asks.

"I'm going to buy a whole pile of books for my daughter," says Father.

"Well, well." The bookseller looks at Anna. "Is it your birthday, young lady?"

"No," her father answers. "She lost all her books when we went into hiding, so she's getting new ones now."

"Hmm . . ." The bookseller coughs.

"May we browse?" Father walks to a bookcase.

"Go ahead, sir. But she must be terribly careful with our books. The publishers won't be able to fill our book orders for a long time. Paper shortage, you understand."

"Anna will certainly be very careful. She loves books."

"Of course I'll be careful," Anna says.

Anna practically dances through the store. Everywhere she looks, she sees books that she used to own.

"Oh, *Kruimeltje* and *The Doppertjes* and . . ."

"Young lady, be quiet, please. You are disturbing the other customers with your shouting. Not so noisy."

Anna looks at the bookseller. "Oh, pardon me," she whispers. "Pardon me, sir.

"There is *Uncle Tom's Cabin*," she whispers to her father.

"Just speak in a normal voice," Papa answers. "Don't worry about what that so-called gentleman says. If he's rude again, I'll come help you."

Anna laughs. She does it quietly, though; otherwise that so-called gentleman will hear her.

"Anna!" Father has a thick book in his hand. "Do you know this one? You *must* read it."

Anna looks at the jacket, which has on it a picture of a boy with a dog. "*Alone in the World*," she reads out loud. "Is it a good book?"

"It's marvelous, really marvelous. I read it for the first time when I was about your age. I don't know how many times I've reread it."

Anna would like to ask more questions, but her father

has opened the book. He doesn't hear Anna or see her, either. He is reading.

"Come on, Papa, let's buy books and leave. I have homework to do."

"One more page. Don't bother me. I'm reading."

"Yes, I can see that." Anna sighs.

"Finished!" Father closes the book. He stands still with the book in his hands.

"Come on," says Anna.

Papa doesn't answer. He looks at the door. A man has just entered the bookstore.

"No!" her father shouts. He raises *Alone in the World* and hurls it at the door. It lands at the man's feet with a thud.

"Stay where you are!" shouts her father. "Stay where you are, you scoundrel!" He turns to Anna. "Wait here. I've got to go after that fellow!"

Father tries to run out of the store, but the bookseller is standing in the doorway with *Alone in the World* in his hand. "Stop," he says.

"Let me go!" Father attempts to push the bookseller aside. "I've got to chase that fellow. He sold *Folk and Fatherland* during the war."

"I don't care," the bookseller replies. "You'll have to pay for the book first. You've ruined it."

"*Folk and Fatherland*," her father calls loudly. "That man sold an N.S.B. newspaper right on the street. Because of people like him, my wife and I had to hide for years in a forest, under the ground. And a person like that is allowed to go free!"

"Stop, Papa." Anna tries to hold him back. "Don't start a fight."

"Let me go, Anna!" Again he tries to push the bookseller out of the way.

"Pay first," says the man. "You people certainly have a lot of nerve. Speaking without thinking, are you? You Jews didn't learn much during the war, did you? You damned Jews!"

Never in her life has Anna seen her father so angry. He raises his arms. She tries to stop him, but she isn't quick enough; he punches the bookseller right in the middle of his face. His gold-rimmed glasses land on the floor, next to Anna. She bends down to pick them up.

"No!" her father shouts. "Let him get them himself."

The bookseller picks up his glasses. "The police," he gasps. "I'm going to call the police."

"Good, I'll wait." Father puts his hands on his sides. "Hurry up. I'll wait until the police come, but they'd better come quickly."

The bookseller rubs his cheek, then walks to the telephone. He looks back at Anna and her father.

"And now we'll wait, Anna," Father says.

She hardly dares to look at the door. The police will be coming soon. She and her father will be taken to the police station, and perhaps will be interrogated and even tortured. During the war, people were tortured until they lost consciousness. Why doesn't Papa leave? Why don't they flee?

"Come on, Papa," Anna whispers. "Let's run away."

"Run away? Don't you understand at all, Anna? I haven't done anything to run away from. I've made it clear to a person that I won't be called names, that he can't just say anything he wants to. Sweetheart, in the past five years I haven't had a chance as splendid as this one."

"Bravo!" calls a woman. "You have my blessing. That was a fine thing you just did."

"Pitiful," says an old man. "Pitiful, such a hot-tempered father? My father was like that, too, but he's been dead for years. There they are. There are the police."

Two policemen enter the store. Anna puts her hands over her eyes.

"Who hit whom?" she hears.

"I did," says her father.

Anna uncovers her eyes.

"I hit *him*." Father points to the bookseller. "He said terrible things about us . . . about Jews."

"Is what this person stated true?" asks a policeman. "I shall make an official report. I shall take all the information down in minute detail." He takes a fountain pen and a small book from the pocket of his uniform.

"I didn't say anything out of the ordinary," says the bookseller. "I only said that the Jews didn't learn anything during the war and . . ."

"So," says the officer to the bookseller. "Is that what you said?"

"Yes, that's what I said."

"Then I'm not going to write anything more. I'm putting my book back in my pocket. My colleague may do what he wishes, but I'm finished here."

"I'm finished, too," says the other officer. He turns to Father. "Do you know what you should do, Mr. uh . . ."

"Markus."

"You should file a complaint against this person because he insulted you, Mr. Markus. Our friend the bookseller will then have to pay a stiff fine, and perhaps he'll even go to jail if the judge deems it necessary. You and your daughter may come along with me." He walks to the door. Anna and her father walk with him.

The officer bows deeply, then points outside. "Go on," he says. "Enjoy the outdoors, for if you endured what I think you did, you haven't been able to enjoy the outdoors nearly enough. Look out . . . duck!"

The officer ducks. Anna and her father duck, too. Something comes whizzing past. They hear a crack. *Alone in the World* is lying in front of them on the sidewalk.

"Ah, our friend the bookseller is a bit angry," says the officer. "He is throwing merchandise from his store. Here, keep it. I know that it's against the law, but you may take the book with you." He gives it to Anna. "What is your name?"

"Anna."

"Good, Anna. Give the book back to me for a minute." The officer flips through the book. "I see. Four guilders and fifty cents. I'll pay the bookseller for the book. May I? I'm going to write something on the first page for you."

He takes the fountain pen from his pocket again and begins to write in the book.

"Here you are," he says. "Read what I've written when you're at home. I've got to go back into the store." He salutes Anna and her father.

"Thank you, sir," she says.

After they have walked a bit, Father says, "Stop, Anna. I don't understand how it happened. I don't understand myself at all. In the past I did that when I was called names. I fought back then, too, but now . . ."

"You hid in a forest. Now I know."

"Yes, we hid in a forest, under the ground. But let's not talk about it, Anna. Not yet. Not everything all at once."

"Shall we look?" she asks.

"Yes, I'm as curious as you are."

Anna opens the book and reads what the policeman inscribed in a beautifully formed script:

> For Anna Markus, the girl who fortunately
> is not alone in the world.
>
> > Sincerely yours,
> > Officer Van Wijk

Anna is going to the Draaikolk today, and it won't cost her a thing. She is going to use one of the tickets that Mrs. Neumann gave her.

"Young lady, your ticket, please," says the guard at the gate.

Anna reaches into her pocket and hands him the rolled-up ticket.

"Oh, how sloppy, all rolled up like that," he says. "Go on. It's crowded. I think that all the schools in Holland have planned to take trips today. They're coming from everywhere. From Groningen, from Brabant . . . everywhere."

"When will the family swing be unveiled?" she asks.

"A week from today," the guard replies. "Exactly a week."

"I'll be back then. I still have another ticket."

"Wonderful, young lady. I'll watch for you."

It is so crowded that Anna can't see the swing or the merry-go-round. There are people everywhere. What Anna *can* see is a large object under a cloth. It looks like a building with a white sheet draped over it.

"What's under that big white cover?" she hears a child ask.

"That's the family swing. We'll be able to go on it next week," the child's mother answers.

Luckily the puppet show is less crowded. Seats are still available on one of the long benches.

"It's nice just to sit here and watch the puppet show," Anna says to a little girl next to her.

"Are Jan Klaassen and Katrijn coming?" the child asks.

"Oh yes, and the witch and the . . ." Anna stops speaking in midsentence.

She looks at the child closely. She knows her; Anna is certain of it, but where has she seen her? Those brown eyes . . .

"There is Jan Klaassen." The little girl folds her arms over her chest.

"What's your name?" Anna *must* ask.

"Jan Klaassen has a big nose," says the child.

Anna is silent. Jan Klaassen and Katrijn are moving before her eyes, but she doesn't hear what they are saying to each other. She keeps glancing to the side, to the little girl. Everyone begins to clap. Now Anna can talk to the child again.

"Ho, ho!" calls Jan Klaassen. "I still have something to say to Katrijn and to the landlord. Don't go away, children!"

"Boo!" shout the children.

The little girl has unfolded her arms and is now sitting with her hands between her legs. "I have to go to the bathroom," she says.

"Come on," Anna says, "I'll go with you."

Together they walk to the bathroom. There is a long line of children waiting to get in.

"Come with me, I know where there's another bathroom," Anna says.

The other bathroom is less crowded. They hardly have to wait at all.

Anna remains outside. That child . . . she knows! She saw that child in Frank van Berkel's movie. That little girl is Fannie. It *must* be Fannie! She has the same curls as Fannie and she has a birthmark on her forehead. Just like the child in the movie.

"Finished." The little girl comes toward Anna. "My pants don't feel right," she says.

"I'll help you," Anna says, and she straightens the child's pants. "Is that better?"

"Yes," she answers.

"What's your name?" Anna asks.

"My name is Lotje. Lotje Schols."

"Say it again. Schols, I mean."

"Schols, Schols, Schols," the child says.

Anna can hear that Lotje's accent is different from her own; she probably lives in a different part of Holland, too.

"Where do you live?"

"In Sittard. Very far . . . in Limburg. We came in a Canadian troop carrier. It was fun riding in an open truck. Long seats to sit on and . . ."

"Are you alone?"

"No, I'm with a class. I was allowed to come by myself

to see the puppet show. A fifth grader will be picking me up later. I'm in the first grade. My father is the school principal and that's why I'm allowed to go on these field trips. I'm coming next week, too. Then I can ride on the family swing."

"How old are you?"

"Seven. I turned seven in the winter. Shall I tell you when?"

"Yes, tell me."

"On the last day of January."

Anna nearly faints. That's right! Fannie's birthday is on January 31, too. "Born on the same day as Princess Beatrix," is what Mrs. Neumann said.

This child is Fannie!

"And do you know what my papa and mama gave me for my birthday?"

"No."

"Wait." Lotje unbuttons the top button of her blouse. She is looking for something.

"This," she says. "Pretty, isn't it?" A little cross on a gold chain is lying in her hand. "Jesus hung on a cross," she continues. "On a bigger cross, though. Jesus was much bigger. I'll put it away now. 'Bye, cross, back you go!"

"Lotje!" calls someone in the distance. "Are you coming?"

"Quick, push your hair back off your forehead," Anna urges her. Anna wants to see Lotje's birthmark again.

"I'm coming!" Lotje shouts, and to Anna she says, "I have to go. They're calling me."

The child runs in the direction of the puppet show.

"See you next week!" says Anna.

Anna can't move. That child . . . she knows it for sure. It's Fannie. But her name is Schols and she is wearing a cross. She is Catholic.

"A false name," Anna says to herself. "And that cross doesn't mean anything, either."

What should she do? Should she run to Mrs. Neumann and say, "I've found Fannie"?

"Where is she?" Mrs. Neumann would ask.

"I don't know."

"You don't *know*? Anna, why didn't you . . ."

Anna doesn't want to think about it anymore. She will have to wait until next week. There is nothing else to be done. Next week she will see Fannie again and then she will say: "Now tell me the truth. I know that you're Fannie."

And what if Fannie is frightened? What if Fannie refuses to talk about it?

Anna's thoughts are all running together. She doesn't know what to do anymore. Should she tell her father and mother? What if it isn't true? What if she has made a mistake and it isn't Fannie? That would make her parents very unhappy.

What should she do?

* * *

Anna doesn't want to stay at the Draaikolk any longer. She wants to go home. It is so crowded that she has difficulty reaching the exit.

"Leaving already?" asks the guard.

"Yes, I'm going," Anna replies.

"You're not coming back next week, are you? You've seen how crowded it is."

"Of course I'm coming," she answers. "Fannie is coming, too."

"That will be nice for you," he says.

◆ *Fannie?*

Anna hasn't been able to sleep for seven nights. For seven nights she has seen Fannie before her eyes.

She has been hearing voices, too: "It *was* Fannie . . . It *wasn't* Fannie . . . You should have asked. Stupid Anna!"

And so it went for seven nights.

"You don't look well, Anna. I'm worried about you," her mother told her.

"Today I'm going to make an appointment for you with Dr. Van Biezen," her father said.

"You should spend more time outside, Anna. You're so pale and you've been so quiet this past week," Mrs. Neumann said.

It was all Anna could do to keep from screaming, "It's because of Fannie! I saw Fannie and I didn't tell anyone!"

All this thinking about Fannie has got to stop. It's driving Anna crazy!

"Oh, so you've come again?" the guard says to Anna. He is wearing a uniform now, a blue one with gold buttons on the jacket and gold stripes on the pants.

"Today is even busier than it was last week," he continues. "You're a clever girl if you can get near the family swing. Wait a minute. I have an idea. The mayor will be coming soon. He'll be following the marching band. Just walk along behind him and pretend you're part of the ceremony. Everyone will think that you're the mayor's daughter. Do you know why I've been talking to you so much?"

"No."

"I know you a little bit. Didn't you wear a star during the war?"

"Yes."

"That's why I've been talking to you, and that's why I think you should stand in front. Don't you think so, too?"

"Yes."

"You're not saying much today. Is your friend coming?"

"Who?"

"Your friend, Fannie. Last week . . ."

"Don't know."

"Have you two been quarreling?"

Anna can't answer. She is cringing, for she hears shooting in the distance.

"Don't be frightened," says the guard. "You hear the band. Drums."

"Oh," says Anna.

The musicians march through the gate, playing drums and horns and copper cymbals.

"Nice, isn't it?" exclaims the guard. Fortunately he doesn't wait for Anna to reply; she doesn't think the music is nice at all.

"Go ahead," says the guard. "Walk behind the band." She walks behind the mayor, who is waving to the crowd.

The musicians come to a halt at the family swing.

"And now I ask you, Honorable Mayor, to unveil the largest swing in Holland," says a man in a strange, long coat.

Anna looks all around her. Where is Fannie? She doesn't recognize any of the children who are standing among the musicians.

". . . And I hereby declare that the largest swing in Holland can be used by all children," proclaims the mayor.

"Long live the mayor. Three cheers for the Draaikolk!" calls the man in the peculiar coat.

Fannie isn't here. She will never be found again.

"Hooray!" A wave of people begins to push toward the swing. Anna is shoved aside. What she wants to do most of all is throw herself on the ground and cry. Cry about everything.

She doesn't even bother to wipe her tears away.

"Are you crying? Look, you've got tears on your cheeks."

Anna feels a little hand slip into her hand.

Fannie!

"Hello, Fannie," says Anna.

"My name is Lotje. Lotje Schols. Will you go on the big swing with me?"

"Yes, Lotje." Anna can hardly answer fast enough.

"I told my papa that I wanted to go on the swing with you. He says it's all right if I do. He saw you standing behind the mayor. Look, there is my papa."

"Come on, Lotje," says Anna. "We'll try to find a place together on the swing."

"If you hurry up you can still get on!" a big boy calls to them.

"*No!*" another boy yells, and he points to Anna. "That bitch can't. She wore a star during the war. I'm not letting any dirty Jews on this swing!"

Anna lets go of Lotje's hand and runs away. She is being called names again, just as she was during the war.

"Don't cry." Anna hears a small voice next to her.

"Go back to the swing, Lotje," Anna replies. "I was the one being called names, not you."

"Come here with your ear. I have something to say into your ear."

Anna bows her head to the child.

"I'm Jewish, too, but I'm not supposed to tell anyone. My father and mother are dead. They were taken away by German soldiers. I'd be dead, too, but my real father pushed me onto the balcony, and the soldiers didn't find me when they came inside. And then someone I didn't know took me to Limburg and that's where I live, with my new father and mother. And now I'm going to go to the bathroom."

She begins to walk away, but Anna stops her. "Come with me," she says to Lotje. "There are long lines waiting to get into the bathrooms. I know of another bathroom you can use, and it's not far from here." She begins to pull Lotje along.

"All right, but let me tell my father first. There he is. Papa, this girl is going to take me to the bathroom."

"Fine, will you take good care of her, as you did last week?" Lotje's father asks.

"Of course," she answers.

"Lotje told me all about you. That's why I'm letting you take her now. Where are you going?"

"To the Vlietkade!" Anna calls.

"Come on!" Anna says to Lotje, and she takes her by the hand. "Run!"

"Not so fast," the child gasps. "I'll wet my pants."

"A little farther . . . and stop. Here we are!"

They are at Mrs. Neumann's house. Anna's hands are shaking so much that she can hardly grasp the key.

"Go inside," she says to Lotje when she has finally opened the door.

"Aren't you coming with me? I don't know where the bathroom is."

"I'll be there in a minute. Go up the stairs and call as loudly as you can: 'Here I am!'"

"Here I am? That's crazy." She looks at Anna with wide eyes.

"Just do it, Lotje. Go in." Anna pushes her into the hall.

Amalia sneaks outside.

"You come with me!" Lotje calls.

"Can't. The cat has gotten out. I have to catch the cat." Anna closes the door softly.

She sits on the fence and stares at the water. There are ships passing by. The people on one of the ships are waving, but Anna doesn't wave back.

Soon the door will open. What will happen then?

"What do you think, Amalia? Is it Fannie?"

Amalia rubs her head against Anna's feet.

Anna is too restless to remain on the fence. She slips off and begins to walk back and forth. She can hear the band playing in the distance.

"It's warm outside, isn't it, Amalia? Warm and cold." She has ice-cold hands and feet.

It is taking Lotje a very long time. Her father is going to be worried about her.

* * *

The door opens.

"All right, I'm finished," Lotje will say when she comes outside. "Let's go back to my father now."

Anna is becoming dizzy. Mrs. Neumann's house is beginning to sway.

There is Lotje.

She is not alone. A woman is standing next to her, a woman wearing a flaming-red dress. Her long hair is bound back in a red velvet ribbon.

They walk toward Anna hand in hand.

"Mrs. Neumann," Anna whispers. "Mrs. Neumann."

"Anna, I'd like you to meet my daughter. This is Fannie. This is Fannie Neumann."

✦ Anna's Letter

Wednesday

Dear Kiki,

I know that you don't really exist. I also know that you can't read letters, but I wanted to write to you, anyway. I'll just put this letter in my desk. Then I can read it whenever I want.

I'm writing this letter to tell you what happened when

I found Fannie. That was a week ago today. I'm still very, very happy.

What did I say . . . happy? I'm so proud I could burst, but I don't want anyone to know that. I'll tell you all about it now.

Fannie, Mrs. Neumann, and I went to the Draaikolk. Mrs. Neumann walked with an arm around each of us. Mr. Schols was waiting by the gate as we arrived. He said that he was very worried because Lotje had been gone for such a long time.

Mrs. Neumann walked up to Mr. Schols and told him who she was. I think that he was terribly shocked. At first he didn't say a word. Then he said that he was very happy for Lotje that she had found her mother.

Mr. Schols asked me to take care of Lotje for a while because he had something important to discuss with Mrs. Neumann. (He kept calling Fannie "Lotje.") The two of them walked a little way from us. I saw them talking, but I couldn't hear what they were talking about. I think I saw both of them crying.

When they returned to us they said that Mrs. Neumann was going to Limburg with them for a couple of days to talk about what they should do next. Mrs. Neumann asked me to lock her front door, and so I did.

It was a strange day, a sort of dream day, and when I stood in front of the empty white house I felt very much alone.

Mrs. Neumann returned from Limburg yesterday. They

discussed many things there. They think it would be better for Fannie not to come live with her real mother right away. She will be staying in Limburg with her foster parents until Christmas vacation. In January she will come to live with Mrs. Neumann for good. Mrs. Neumann says that they have already grown a bit used to each other during those days in Limburg. Fannie will visit her mother every weekend, and I've been invited to come, too, but I don't know yet if I want to. I'm allowed to keep Mrs. Neumann's key.

Mrs. Neumann still had her red dress on when she returned yesterday. She had the velvet ribbon in her hair, too. I think that she is so pretty now. She was very, very happy, she said. I can understand why!

Kiki, you know a whole lot of news now. I'm going to stop.

Love,
Anna

P.S. Mrs. Neumann and I are going downtown this afternoon. She is going to buy me a book. It doesn't matter if the book is expensive, Mrs. Neumann says. She's going to inscribe something in the book for me, something nice, she says.

P.S. On Saturday Fannie will be coming to spend the weekend with Mrs. Neumann. I'll give her the silver coin bracelet then. How happy she'll be!

P.S. Mrs. Neumann told me that Mr. and Mrs. Schols

are terribly sad that Fannie will be going away in January. They saved her life, and they love her very much.

Mrs. Neumann promised that they may come visit Fannie as often as they like. Fannie said that she loves Mr. and Mrs. Schols very much, and that she will visit them often, too. Even later on, when she is older.

I'm going to hide this letter, because my father and mother will think that I'm crazy to be writing to someone who doesn't exist. Grown-ups don't understand things like that.

Goodbye, dear Kiki.

Love,
Anna